Cry of the Banshee

Also From Heather Graham

Krewe of Hunters series
Phantom Evil
Heart of Evil
Sacred Evil
The Evil Inside
The Unseen
The Unholy
The Unspoken
The Uninvited
The Night is Watching
The Night is Alive
The Night is Forever
The Cursed
The Hexed
The Betrayed
The Silenced
The Forgotten
The Hidden
Haunted Destiny
Deadly Fate
Darkest Journey
Dying Breath
Dark Rites
Wicked Deeds
Fade to Black
Pale As Death
Echoes of Evil
Christmas, the Krewe and a Large White Rabbit
The Summoning
The Seekers
The Stalking
Seeing the Darkness
Deadly Touch
Dreaming Death
Horror-Ween
The Best Christmas Ever
Sound of Darkness

Aura of Night
Voice of Fear

Other Books by Heather Graham

A Dangerous Game
A Perfect Obsession
Flawless
Waking the Dead
Let the Dead Sleep
Night of the Vampires
The Keepers
Ghost Moon
Ghost Night
Ghost Shadow
The Killing Edge
Night of the Wolves
Home in Time for Christmas
Unhallowed Ground
Dust to Dust
Nightwalker
Deadly Gift
Deadly Harvest
Deadly Night
The Death Dealer
The Last Noel
The Séance
Blood Red
The Dead Room
Kiss of Darkness
The Vision
The Island
Ghost Walk
Killing Kelly
The Presence
Dead on the Dance Floor
Picture Me Dead
Haunted
Hurricane Bay
A Season of Miracles
Night of the Blackbirds

Never Sleep with Strangers
Eyes of Fire
Slow Burn
Night Heat
Danger in Numbers
Crimson Summer

From 1001 Dark Nights
Crimson Twilight
When Irish Eyes Are Haunting
All Hallow's Eve
Blood on the Bayou
Hallow Be The Haunt
Haunted Be the Holidays
Blood Night
The Dead Heat of Summer
Haunted House
Descend to Darkness
Cry of the Banshee

Cry of the Banshee

A Krewe of Hunters Novella

By Heather Graham

1001 DARK NIGHTS
PRESS

Cry of the Banshee
A Krewe of Hunters Novella

ISBN: 979-8-88542-045-7

Published by 1001 Dark Nights Press, an imprint of Evil Eye Concepts, Incorporated

Sign up for the 1001 Dark Nights Newsletter
and be entered to win a Tiffany Key necklace.

There's a contest every month!

Go to www.1001DarkNights.com to subscribe.

As a bonus, all subscribers can download
FIVE FREE exclusive books!

One Thousand and One Dark Nights

Once upon a time, in the future…

I was a student fascinated with stories and learning. I studied philosophy, poetry, history, the occult, and the art and science of love and magic. I had a vast library at my father's home and collected thousands of volumes of fantastic tales.

I learned all about ancient races and bygone times. About myths and legends and dreams of all people through the millennium. And the more I read the stronger my imagination grew until I discovered that I was able to travel into the stories... to actually become part of them.

I wish I could say that I listened to my teacher and respected my gift, as I ought to have. If I had, I would not be telling you this tale now. But I was foolhardy and confused, showing off with bravery.

One afternoon, curious about the myth of the Arabian Nights, I traveled back to ancient Persia to see for myself if it was true that every day Shahryar (Persian: شهريار, "king") married a new virgin, and then sent yesterday's wife to be beheaded. It was written and I had read that by the time he met Scheherazade, the vizier's daughter, he'd killed one thousand women.

Something went wrong with my efforts. I arrived in the midst of the story and somehow exchanged places with Scheherazade – a phenomena that had never occurred before and that still to this day, I cannot explain.

Now I am trapped in that ancient past. I have taken on Scheherazade's life and the only way I can protect myself and stay alive is to do what she did to protect herself and stay alive.

Every night the King calls for me and listens as I spin tales. And when the evening ends and dawn breaks, I stop at a point that leaves him breathless and yearning for more. And so the King spares my life for one more day, so that he might hear the rest of my dark tale.

As soon as I finish a story... I begin a new one... like the one that you, dear reader, have before you now.

Prologue

A Cry in the Night

At first, Moira Hawkins thought she might be imagining the sound. It was so soft at first, like a sigh on the wind or a whisper through the trees.

Except she wasn't in the woods. She was lying in bed in the private wing of Castle Darien, her family's nearly ancient stronghold.

But the windows were open. That had to be it. The temperature was cool but pleasant, and she didn't need to use the heat or air-conditioning systems. Which was good since they would never be great in such an old stone fortress.

Moira had promised her grandmother she wouldn't let the castle, built at the end of the thirteenth century, go to ruin. She said she would do everything needed to bring it up to the standards so many others used to save the structure and turn it into a hotel.

She was partway there. While she worked on getting the necessary loans and finding contractors to undertake such an epic restructuring, she hired a tour company to bring visitors through. There were even a few *Haunted Ireland* tours put on by historians, who talked about some of the dire events of the Emerald Isle's bloody past.

She figured anything around for over eight-hundred years must have some nightmarish events to relay.

And her ancestral home was in the Republic of Ireland, which had suffered a great deal of bloodshed to get where it was today.

Yet…

It occurred to her that she had heard—or at least imagined—the soft, mournful sobs before.

The night Granny had died.

Imagination. Had to be.

But she'd heard the sound the night before they found the old man drowned in the river that ran alongside the castle's western wall, too.

And the time the would-be thief fell to his death from the wall.

They'd learned the elderly gentleman, visiting family in the area, had been suffering from cancer. Moira wondered if he had chosen his end.

And while the thief shouldn't have been trying to climb the wall, he hadn't deserved death.

As she thought back, she realized the sound had preceded all those events.

She shook her head. She had to be imagining it. She might have spent the last few years of Granny's illness working in the States, but she'd grown up with all the tales of leprechauns, pixies, fairies, and banshees. Granny had been so good at telling them, holding her cousins and her spellbound as she wove her magical tales.

The crying grew louder. She *wasn't* imagining it. She could definitely hear it.

It wasn't a frightened cry. It was mournful, heartfelt. Yet *Moira* was afraid.

Where is it coming from?

She glanced at the clock on her bedside table—just past midnight.

The last ghost tour had ended by now, but she wasn't alone in the castle. Stewart McKenna, her grandmother's longtime castle steward, slept down the hall with his wife. Their son's bedroom was next door to theirs. Nellie Antrim, the head housekeeper, was on this floor, as well. And while the tour of the two unoccupied towers had just ended, Mark Meadows, the tour agency's director, often stayed behind to answer any questions the guests might have regarding the castle or Ireland's history. Because, of course, Mark wasn't just a businessman, though he was a good one. He truly loved history and didn't mind working late. He was…wonderful.

The sobbing continued.

Moira's mind went to something her granny had told her.

Banshee. Banshees are the remains of the Tuatha dé Danann, the gods of Ireland, driven underground when the Milesians arrived—Gaels who traveled the Earth, seeking a home. And there, in Éire, they claimed the land while the Tuatha dé Danann settled the underworld. Once, keeners *had been on hand at funerals, sobbing mournfully for those who had left the earthly world. The banshees fulfilled that tradition now, warning of someone's death…*

Get a grip! she told herself. Seriously, she'd spent enough time in the United States to learn all about all kinds of myths and legends from around the world.

There are no such things as banshees.

Still…

She leapt out of bed, determined to dress quickly and find out what was happening. Stewart was only rooms away, and if she ran across the great hall that separated her from the Great Tower, she was sure she'd find Mark lingering.

She was being ridiculous. Of course, she'd never expected to come home to Ireland, only to sit by her beloved Granny's side until her departure, then be charged with saving their ancestral home. She hadn't thought of herself as an extreme coward, but then again…

She wasn't a cop or an enforcer of the law. She'd been an actress, for God's sake.

Act brave! she told herself.

But bravery fled quickly.

About as fast as she ran out of her room.

The other doors in the occupied Darien Tower were closed. Neither Stewart nor any of the others seemed to have heard the wailing.

She tore across the expansive hallway, lined with crests and paintings of the great Darien family members from the last eight-hundred-plus years, to the Great Tower. She sped down the ancient stone staircase to the ground floor and the massive audience hall, to find that Mark was still there, chatting with a group of five people. *Americans,* she thought: two young couples, one with a teenager.

"Moira," Mark said, curious but smiling as he greeted her. "Friends, this is a special occasion, indeed. Moira Hawkins is the castle's owner."

"It's amazing," a young woman said.

"Magnificent," echoed her husband.

"So, so, cool!" exclaimed the teenage boy at their side.

Moira smiled weakly. "Thank you so much. The castle has survived much, but you've been with one of the most amazing historians I know."

Mark Meadows was relatively young. He'd been born in Chicago, Illinois, to Irish immigrants who continually returned to Dublin to visit family. He had attended Trinity College and then opened his tour company soon after graduating with a history degree. He was thirty now, she knew, having investigated him before they drew up their contract. And he had a stellar reputation for telling straight history and the legends and myths surrounding it. Tall, fit, dark-haired, and blue-eyed, he was a handsome and charming man who was great at his chosen work. He had other guides working for him, but she was glad he was the one here tonight.

Someone she knew. Someone with whom she was…close.

And yet…

The way he smiled told her he hadn't heard the sobbing. He likel
wondered why the hell she was still up when she usually went to bed b
eleven and was up by seven or eight to begin work on the renovations.

"Lovely to have you here," she told the group. She shrugged as
merely curious or perhaps amused, then said, "I thought I heard someon
crying. It must have been the wind. But I just wanted to make sur
everything was all right."

Mark looked at her curiously. "We're just waiting for one of ou
group members to return from the facilities," he told her. "And thes
lovely people had a few questions. We had quite a group tonight. Almos
thirty. The others have departed, but we're waiting on Mrs. Robertson t
rejoin us. Once she returns, I will, of course, lock the tower for the night.

Mark never failed to lock up, and he and his employees checked i
and out with the officer at the gatehouse for every tour. Naturally, h
wouldn't deny a guest in need, but neither would he leave the premise
without ensuring every member of his tour group was out of the castle.

Moira suddenly heard the loud sobbing again as if coming fror
above—or the air around her.

Yet no one else seemed to hear it.

She smiled and looked at the others. Nothing. No reaction fror
them at all.

"Mrs. Robertson has been gone a while now," Mark murmured. "I
uh—"

"I'll run up and check on her," Moira assured him.

Was she hearing things? She remembered how she had listened wide
eyed to Granny as she talked about the leprechauns, their gold, the wa
they loved to play practical jokes…and, of course, the banshees, keenin
and wailing in warning or to take some of the pain from those th
deceased left behind.

Moira smiled and hurried up the old stone stairs. They'd managed t
put in a lift to adhere to ADA regulations, but she just wanted to ge
upstairs to the modern—well, almost modern—restroom Granny had pu
in about twenty years ago to make the tower accommodating to tourists.

"Mrs. Robertson?" Moira called as she opened the restroom door.

She really hoped she wouldn't need to look in the three stalls.

She didn't need to. The keening burst into a loud sob, and Moira sav
the woman on the floor by the sinks.

Loud. So very loud.

"Mrs. Robertson!" Moira cried, sinking down next to the woman.

Her eyes were closed. Moira sought a pulse and found none. The woman wasn't breathing.

She yelled for help, but there was no help for this, and she knew it.

The woman was dead.

And the banshee had tried her best to warn Moira.

Chapter 1

Jackson Crow, Supervising Field Agent for the subtitled *Krewe of Hunters* unit of the FBI, looked up as his wife and second-in-command, Angela Hawkins-Crow, pushed open his office door.

He peered at her expectantly. They generally used their phones when they needed to communicate about a case. Not that he wasn't happy to see her. It was pretty amazing that they worked together, but then the Krewe was a pretty amazing thing in and of itself.

"Angela? Come on in."

The look on her face showed concern and disconcertment. At first, he'd been afraid that something had happened to one of their children, teenage Corby or little Victoria, but he knew Angela wouldn't be so calm if that were the case.

"What is it?" he asked her, concerned and disconcerted himself.

She walked the rest of the way in and sat in front of his desk. For a minute, he remembered their first case in New Orleans and how he had admired her for her work ethic and ability. That had quickly turned to love. Angela was professional, and even all these years later, she was still one of the most stunning women he had ever met with her swath of long hair and bright, always-caring eyes.

She leaned forward. "How do you feel about a trip to Ireland?"

He sat back, curious. "Angela, we have a European division now—"

"But this is personal."

"In Ireland?"

She nodded slowly. "Okay. So…you know I have a cousin—second cousin or cousin once removed, whatever—from my mom's side.

Anyway, to make a long story short—"

"Too late." Jackson grinned.

"Right. My mom's mom was a Darien. And while we weren't in line to inherit, though I wouldn't have wanted to be in the running, there *is* a Castle Darien about an hour from Dublin."

"Wait. I remember. Pretty girl, pretty name. Moira. We went to lunch with her when she was back in the States to tie up some loose ends here. An actress, right? She came to redo a few shots for a commercial or something."

Angela nodded. "Yes. Moira. She was in tears and begged me to come. Me. Not a stranger, Jackson."

"Why? What happened?"

Angela let out a long sigh. "Okay, so, she inherited Castle Darien from her beloved grandmother, the direct heiress. And she—"

"Is she a lady? A princess? Or—?"

"I believe she is addressed as *lady*, but the real titles were lost long ago. The point is, she's afraid she's losing her mind. She heard a banshee crying, and then her grandmother died. She heard it again when some accidents happened at the castle. And then—"

"Accidents?"

"An elderly man drowned in the river, and then a would-be thief fell off the wall."

"Sad, but—"

"Now, they found one of their tourists dead in the ladies' room."

"Okay…" he said slowly.

"Jackson, she thinks the woman was murdered this time. She was a perfectly healthy American tourist when she walked into the castle, a woman of only thirty-eight. And Moira found her dead of an apparent heart attack."

"Not common, but it can happen—"

"She had no history of heart problems."

"But still—"

"Jackson, please. It's fairly quiet right now, and when we need to be away, the McFadden brothers handle the office just fine in our absence. It's nice to think we're indispensable, but that isn't true of anyone anywhere."

He lowered his head for a minute and then nodded, grinning.

He looked up at her. "Hey, what's not to like about Ireland?"

She smiled. "I was hoping you'd say that. Of course, we'll have to reach some officials here to get clearance for a more in-depth autopsy, talk to Amelia Robertson's family, and—"

"You think she was murdered? Why? Why would someone murder an American tourist outside of Dublin?"

"Moira believes the banshee warned her, but she didn't listen fast enough. She can't tell anyone, but she's sure that's what happened, and something evil is in her ancestral home. Jackson, we can help her."

He nodded. "Okay. You have a bag here, right?"

"Always."

"I'll call Adam and get the ball rolling on the documents and help we'll need, and—"

"I'll call Mary Tiger and have her apologize to the kids for us and tell them we'll be back as soon as possible."

He nodded again. She rose, ready to return to her office, make her calls, and grab her go bag, something they all kept because they were based out of the DC area but traveled the country when necessary.

He put his calls through, first to Adam Harrison, their founder, an amazing philanthropist and great man. He'd lost his beloved son when Josh was only a teen. But instead of growing bitter, Adam put his efforts into solving strange cases with people who were academy graduates, law enforcement, and *gifted* in interesting ways.

Like speaking with the dead who remained and had something to say.

As usual, Adam seemed capable of performing magic. They were good to go. And Bruce McFadden was ready to grab the reins. Jackson assured him he'd be in touch throughout their time in Ireland, and Bruce nodded grimly.

That was it.

Within an hour, they were in their company jet and on the way to Dublin.

As they flew, Jackson watched Angela looking out the window. The sky was cloudless and blue—a beautiful day to fly. Jackson and Angela sat across from each other in the plane's large, comfortable chairs, and Jackson studied her.

"According to the histories I've read, the Norse founded Dublin," he said, trying to distract her from the worry she clearly felt.

She looked at him and smiled. "I happen to know you're up on world history, so…yeah. Basically. The first Viking raid was circa 1795, then the Vikings started coming more frequently. And, yes, they created a stronghold that became Dublin. They mainly arrived from western Norway. In time, it became a settlement and trading station. Let a few generations pass, and you end up with a mixed people called the *Gall-*

Gaels, Gall being an Irish word for foreigners."

Jackson knew Angela loved giving him history lessons, and he listened as she went over more details. From Elizabeth I and James I hundreds of years ago, to the Great Irish Famine in the nineteenth century, the country had a fascinating history. All circling back to why they were on their way to an Irish castle. Moira may only be a distant cousin, and her situation might be a bit stranger than they usually encountered, but Angela longed to help.

And prevent additional tragedy.

So did he.

When Angela took a breath, he looked at her and smiled. The light in her eyes as she settled into her element made something in his chest warm. He loved his wife, and it didn't matter if they were at home with the kids, on a case, or on a plane discussing the past, she was his perfect partner.

She returned his smile and continued. "Then there was 1914—World War I. The Irish were supposed to be under home rule, but that was suspended because of the war. And then in 1916, there was the Easter Rising and more fighting. The Irish Free State finally came about in 1921, with northern Ireland opting to remain part of Great Britain. Though throughout the years, until fairly recently, there were still uprisings by the Irish Republican Army.

She ran a hand through her hair. "But in the last decades, Ireland has been great. I always wondered if seeing the terror and tragedy of the Twin Towers going down showed the world that terrorism was terrorism, and little children and innocent men and women shouldn't pay for the injustices done by others in years long past."

"Maybe. Who knows?" Jackson murmured. "So, this Castle Darien—"

"Built when the Vikings were down, and the Normans were basically holding power. Interestingly, they were big on castles, so Castle Darien was once a stronghold. And now that we're into the twenty-first century, a castle means only one thing."

"Really expensive upkeep?"

"Yep," Angela said, nodding sagely. "Anyway, Colleen Darien, Moira's grandmother, didn't want to let the castle out of the family, but she knew it would fall into disrepair without all the farming and resources that used to support it. She was planning to renovate it into a hotel—like many other castles in Ireland. But then, she got older and older, and then

sadly passed away. Moira is her direct heir, just as Colleen was the direc
heir beneath her grandmother."

"Hmm. Are other family members trying to steal the inheritanc
from her?" Jackson asked.

"You have such a suspicious mind," Angela said and grinned.

"Comes with the territory," he replied dryly. And it did. In hi
experience, violence could bloom from sudden anger *and* long-festerin
resentment. Homicides occurred because of jealousy, hatred, and/o
greed—greed often being the root of the murder. Of course, there *we*
serial killers out there—human beings with twisted minds who enjoye
the fear and agony they might cause others, as well as the power over lif
and death.

If someone killed Mrs. Robertson, there were two likely scenario
Either they simply wanted her out of the way, or it was an attack on Moir
and Castle Darien.

Angela watched Jackson and grimaced. "I see your mind working,
she told him. "And, seriously, if another heir wants the castle, they're i
for an education. From everything Moira's told me, it's all quite a pain i
the butt. Handling all the historical ramifications properly while finding
way to hold on to the ownership and make the castle a self-sustainin
entity? Moira's other cousins are all distant, like me. Colleen was one o
several children, but all her siblings died young, and their children no
have children. Half of them, like me, have families in other countrie
where they've been for years. No second in line has been ignored."

"That you know about," Jackson said. "Heirs can come out of th
woodwork at times."

Angela frowned. "Seriously. No one has been around foreve
Colleen raised Moira after her folks died in a tragic car accident. And sh
was proud of Moira for being an actress, happy to see her work in th
United States and come home when she could. But when Colleen got il
Moira hurried back to be with her until the end."

"All right," Jackson said. "Say no one is waiting to unseat Moira. Thi
woman may have died of natural causes."

"Maybe. But it's the…"

Her voice trailed off as she looked out the plane's window agair
taking in the endless blue sky now turning dark. They'd left the office jus
after noon, but the night began to settle upon them as they traveled east.

"Banshee," Jackson said.

Angela nodded. "I mean, most people would think you and I and th
Krewe members are certifiable, often getting aid from the dead whe

working on a case. So, who am I to say banshees don't exist?"

"I think you're more worried about Moira's state of mind than you are concerned that someone might have been murdered in your ancestral castle."

"It's both," Angela said and smiled sweetly. "And that's where you come in. You and Adam, of course. I'm willing to bet the standard autopsy that suggested she died of a heart attack didn't test for any poisons."

"And that's always a possibility," Jackson said. He reached out, touching her face. "Angela, we're on the way. We will find the truth."

* * * *

Ireland.

Angela had been here with her parents as a child and even traveled to the Emerald Isle a few times as an adult. She'd known about Castle Darien and had visited when she was young, but hadn't been back in years. Strange, perhaps, when you had a castle in your family, but her life had always been a wee bit different. *She* was a wee bit different.

But she did love Ireland. It truly was lush and green. Dublin was a bustling city, offering wonderful restaurants, nightlife, museums, and more.

And it had rich history.

And charming people. Every human they encountered was cheerful and accommodating, from the time they landed until they picked up their rental car.

By night, the city of Dublin was alive and awash in a sea of lights.

"Do you feel like you're home?" Jackson teased.

"Do *you* feel comfortable driving on the opposite side of the road?" she countered.

Jackson just grinned.

He kept smiling as they left the city behind. The homes and businesses became sparser and then grew the closer they got to Castle Darien.

"Bit of trivia for you. As far as my family goes, the name Darien originated in Scotland—from a French town's name. And while I haven't seen this documented anywhere, according to my family it—"

"Means?" Jackson asked.

"Loyal unto death," Angela said. She shrugged and quirked a lip. "Some claim the first Darien was Robert Fitzgerald Darien of Limerick, circa 1363. Probably a marriage between the Darien Scot and an Irish lass—the original brought through the Norman invasions of the British Isles. History gets lost and confused, so sometimes… Anyway, I'm rambling."

She tucked a piece of hair behind her ear. "Let's hope Mrs. Richardson died of natural causes, and we just get a cool vacation in Ireland at my family's castle."

He laughed. "Sure. Rub it in. You have ties to a family castle."

"I think castles are cool to visit, but there's too much cleaning," she said.

He laughed softly. As he drove, Angela noticed they had messages on their phones.

"Hey, this is from Adam. He's sounds nonchalant, but he worked his magic. An Inspector McCray was called in when Moira found Mrs. Robertson. He's happy to work with us. And, somehow, Adam managed to get new tox screens done on Mrs. Robertson. We'll know soon enough if she had something other than expected in her system that caused her heart attack."

"That's great. Let's hope McCray is open to us being there, and not in a position where he's been forced to work with us. But then again, you know… The luck o' the Irish."

Angela laughed. "My mom's mom used to complain that meant no luck at all. I guess we'll see."

And they did. They approached the castle not long after. Even by night, lit with great spotlights and the glow of the moon, it was truly a remarkable structure with three towers connected by two-story walls with hallways within. A stone wall with a gatehouse and a huge gate encircled the place, the family name fashioned in metal atop it.

Angela watched Jackson as they arrived. It didn't appear that anyone could just sneak into the castle, not with the gatehouse and the gatekeeper.

But she knew what he was likely thinking. Just because something seemed incredibly improbable did not mean it was impossible.

Besides, it remained true that if someone murdered Mrs. Robertson, the killer had been within the castle walls that night.

"What are you thinking?" she asked Jackson as they approached the gatehouse.

"I'm thinking the Normans knew how to build."

Angela smiled. "See what I mean, though? Way too much to clean, and we'd never be able to find the kids."

"Ah, but a pool—"

"In Ireland?"

"They do have warm days. And from what I've heard, the Irish do swim."

She laughed softly. The guard stepped out from the gatehouse.

They had arrived, and it was time to begin.

Chapter 2

"May I help you?" the guard asked. He appeared to be fiftyish, a stocky man of about five-ten with slightly graying hair and a stern expression. But before they could answer, he smiled and said, "Ah, the Americans. The cousin from the States and her husband?"

"Jackson and Angela Crow, yes. And thank you. You were expecting us?" Angela asked.

"Oh, aye. Moira has been so excited and anxious for you to arrive. Samuel Hall here, an officer with Lock-Stone Security. Please forgive me, I didn't mean to be so informal—"

"We like informal," Jackson assured him. "And it's a pleasure to meet you. Were you working the night before last?" he asked.

The guard nodded grimly. "That I was, sir. Such a tragedy. For a young woman to suffer such a fate. Well, I'm glad you're here with Moira now. She is a dear, and we adore her, just as we loved Colleen. Both wanted to survive here and do so by taking care that they preserve the rich history of the place and working with all the right agencies to maintain that which is precious. Anyway, I'll not hold you here. Moira will be happy to see you."

"Thank you," Angela said, watching as he went to open the gate. "But, Samuel, if you don't mind… May we ask if anyone else came through here that night? Anyone beyond the tour group."

"No, they did not. And I would have seen them," he said firmly. "I told the inspector that. I mean, the poor lass died of a heart attack, but the Gardaí here are thorough. They asked me the same question, and I gave them the same assurance. No one else passed through these gates. We keep a log, and we keep a lookout. Our company has an excellent reputation."

"I'm sure it does," Angela told him, smiling sweetly.

"You've the look of her," Samuel said. "Of our Moira."

"We are cousins," Angela said lightly.

"Nay, lady. More in the kindness and care upon your face," he said and nodded with a smile.

Angela returned the gesture. "Pleasure to meet you, sir."

"Sam, if you'd like," he told them and grinned. "We have Dr. Seuss, even here. Sam, I am. And I traveled to Universal Studios, discovering Sam-I-Am and that I like green eggs and ham."

Laughing softly, Angela and Jackson drove ahead as the great gates opened for them.

"Well?" Angela asked her husband.

"Friendly guard," he said.

"Do you believe him?" she asked.

"Yeah, I do. At the very least, I think he believes he's telling the truth that no one else entered."

"These walls are thick, high, and topped with metal spikes," Angela said.

"Interesting. Didn't you say a thief fell from these walls?"

"Dead and buried long ago," Angela confirmed.

"But this woman now? Hmm. Most *probably,* if there was foul play, someone who was supposed to be within these walls at the time created it."

"Which," Angela pointed out, "would put an end to the supposition that another, more distant heir is trying to take the place from Moira."

"Unless they had an accomplice—paid or otherwise," Jackson pointed out.

"You never like anything easy," she said with a sigh.

"And after all these years at this, do you?" he countered.

He was right. Far too often, it was the bizarre, the *what shouldn't have been.*

The great doors to the central tower burst open as Jackson drove the car along the horseshoe drive to the castle.

Moira stepped out.

Angela saw the relief and excitement on her cousin's face and smiled. Moira was truly lovely with sweeping, long, reddish-gold hair, green eyes, and beautiful features. From all Angela knew, she was a good person. She was also on her way up as an actress, having been hired for several commercials and guest spots on series. But she'd come back to Ireland because her grandmother was failing. She longed to act, but in he everyday life, she seemed to have no ego and was in awe that Jackson an Angela were in the FBI and worked to save lives—and when the couldn't, they found justice.

"You're here!" Moira cried excitedly, coming down the steps fron the grand entry. She gave Angela a heartfelt hug and then embrace Jackson as she began to gush. "Thank you. I don't know how you go here so fast, but I've heard you're miracle workers. I've been told they'r going to do an expanded autopsy. I am so grateful. I'd like to believe was only hearing things, and something natural happened. I mear before…we know elderly Mr. Adair drowned, water in his lungs, and can't help but be sorry. And we know the thief crushed his skull when h fell. And I…um, of course, to Granny, a banshee was perfectly natura But then I haven't had any leprechauns running around to give me a po of gold and… Geez, I'm just rambling now." She exhaled loudly and the continued.

"You must be tired. Come on in. Two of the towers, including th Great Tower here, are kept for tours, historical investigations, and th like, but the great hall connects it to the tower we live in—Darien Towe It's a cool place. At one time, they had grand festivities there. Granny sai they kept the prisoners in the third tower. And there is a scar basement—the catacombs are down there. And…I'm *still* rambling." Sh chuckled nervously.

Both Angela and Jackson laughed. "We're just fine, but thanks s much," Angela assured her. "Our boss, Assistant Director Adan Harrison, is the real magician. He was able to get us here quickly."

"Oh, yes. The inspector called me. He said he'd be here aroun nine."

"Good," Angela said.

"Honestly, we're fine," Jackson assured Moira. "We had an eas flight, and I realize it's growing late here."

Moira shrugged. "I've been wide awake waiting for you, so gratef you were coming. But my housekeeper, the castle steward, his wife, an their son *are* sleeping, I think. Of course, I canceled the tours for th night, though the company believes the woman's tragic death was b natural causes."

"Is there a reason you don't think that?" Jackson asked her.

Moira paused, shaking her head and looking genuinely distressed "Something was just…different."

"Different?" Angela pursued gently.

Moira nodded. "Please, you must believe me. I heard the banshee before Granny died, but the sound was just mournful. Not…I don't know how to explain it. This time," she said, hesitating with a wince, "was like before. Like I told you when I asked you to come. When the man drowned, and the thief fell. It sounded as if she were trying to warn me."

"We don't disbelieve you," Angela assured her.

"Anyone else would," Moira insisted. "Even here, where we all hear the stories and legends from the time we're born. Even I can't help but be—"

"Suspicious?" Jackson said, nodding his understanding.

"Afraid," Moira whispered.

"Well, we're here now, and we'll *be* here until this situation is resolved. That's a promise," Jackson said.

Moira managed to smile. "Thank you," she whispered. "Let's head through."

They did. Jackson glanced at Angela as they passed the area Moira had called the great hall. Paintings and plaques bearing coats of arms lined the walls—some with real swords, daggers, and other weapons.

From Jackson's look, Angela knew he was pinpointing the potential dangers in the hallway. It was long and expansive, and Angela could almost envision the elaborate balls and entertainment that might have been held here in the past with dancing, music, and all the things that were the joyous parts of life.

They finally arrived at the household tower, and Moira showed them the lift they would use to reach the second floor.

"I'm a stair person, usually," Moira said. "But with your bags…"

"The lift is fine. But we'd like to do something tonight once we get this stuff into our room," Angela told her.

"Oh?" Moira asked.

"We need to see the bathroom where you found Mrs. Robertson."

Moira lowered her head for a minute but then looked at them, almost as if she'd inwardly squared her shoulders.

"Of course."

She walked some more. "Okay, I put you right next to me. The McKennas—Stewart, the steward, who watches out for maintenance problems and runs the day-to-day needs of the castle, and his wife—are three rooms down that way." She pointed. "They have a twelve-year-old son, Daniel, in the room next to them. Nellie, a true doll who manages all the housekeeping chores and does our cooking, is down there—"

"One person cleans this place?" Jackson asked incredulously.

Moira giggled. "No. But she's in charge of the help we bring in. She's lovely. In her early fifties with the energy of a twenty-year-old. And full of wit and wisdom. She can tell you all things Irish. However, I have you two here, right next to me." She stopped outside a door. "There is a small balcony overlooking the inner courtyard. It's lovely, truly. Shall I give you two time to settle?"

"No, no, we all need some sleep," Jackson said, placing their luggage outside their door. "If it's possible to take a look…?"

They went down some ancient stone steps and across to the Great Tower, then up another set of stairs to a door marked *Women's Toilet.*

Crime scene tape hung haphazardly from it.

"The inspector said they're done. It was…well, at first, we hoped it would be a rescue mission, but I knew. I heard the banshee," Moira said.

Angela nodded to her and looked at Jackson. "Back and the stalls," she told him.

"Front and the sinks," he agreed.

The bathroom was spotless. Angela could smell the strong scent of disinfectant cleaner as she worked, searching the floor, around the toilets, and studying every stall door.

"Where did you find the woman?" Jackson asked Moira.

"Right there. By the sink. It was as if she collapsed while washing her hands."

Jackson nodded and looked at Angela.

"We'll come back tomorrow," he said quietly. "For now…"

"Yep. We'll all be worthless without some rest," Angela said.

"With you two sleeping in the next room, I may actually get some tonight," Moira said.

They headed back to the other tower, and Angela hugged Moira goodnight, reminding her that they were just next door. "Call us anytime. About anything," she told her cousin.

"Trust me, I will. Indeed, I will," Moira assured.

They split apart, and Angela headed into their room. The window drapes were open, and a soft breeze blew in. She walked over and then moved onto the stone balcony. The courtyard below was beautifully planted with trees and flowering bushes. A section was just grass, perhaps for future hotel guests to play croquet or another lawn game. It was all wonderful and peaceful, especially beneath the moon.

"The electric bill here must be a doozy," Jackson commented, stripping off his jacket and coming to stand behind her.

He put his hands on her shoulders, massaged them, and then pulled her closer.

"Aren't you exhausted?" she asked him.

He whispered close to her ear, "I've never made love in a castle."

She smiled and turned in his arms to face him. It was an incredible thing in today's world—thanks to Adam Harrison's amazing powers of giving and creating—that she could be both married to and partnered with a man she admired and adored.

She lifted her chin to meet his eyes.

"We'll likely be here a few days, you know," she whispered.

"Are you that tired?" he asked softly.

"Castle, tent, whatever…if it has a bed—"

"Or doesn't," he teased.

"It doesn't matter to me where we are."

"But a castle?"

She sidled closer to him and ran her fingers through his dark hair. "Hmm," she murmured. "A castle. Like a prince and princess?"

He laughed and softly ran his knuckles down the side of her cheek. "How about an incredible chief and a princess?" he queried.

She paused for a moment, studying him. "You are an extraordinary chief. You turned people who were strangely gifted—or cursed—into a body of investigators who serve across our country and beyond. And by doing so, have saved so many lives."

He shook his head. "Adam has the brilliant mind, the means, and the immense human compassion. He turned us into what we are. And thanks to him, my life is incredible, no matter what we're facing. Because I have you, Corby, and Victoria."

She smiled and inched even closer to him, feeling the beauty of the breeze and the warmth of his arms.

"And the Krewe of Hunters gave us Mary, who is amazing. Which means we can leave and fool around in a castle while doing our due diligence at work."

He laughed. "Okay, let's quit patting ourselves on the back and—"

"Pat ourselves in a few other places?" she teased.

"That will work. All right, the prince and the princess in the tower."

"I think it was always *Lord* and *Lady so and so* or—"

"Whatever." He swept her into his arms dramatically. "I'm rescuing the princess from the tower," he claimed.

"Oh, yeah? You know this princess can rescue herself, right?"

"Crack shot and expert in several martial arts. I don't intend to fight with this princess," he assured her. "There are so many better things we can do."

She laughed as they left the balcony, crashed onto the bed, and struggled to remove the Glocks they'd managed to receive permission to carry before shedding their shoes and clothing. Each removal came with another whisper of breath, a kiss, or a caress. By the time their guns were on the nightstands and their clothing was strewn everywhere, they were half-laughing, half-urgent, and almost desperate to make love.

As they did, Angela marveled at the sensations, the physical beauty that could rise between the two of them. Somewhere in the back of her mind, she was aware that it was always strangely comfortable yet new, as if they'd both just discovered the absolute wonder of being together for the first time.

She had been incredibly lucky in life. She had married a man who had become her best friend and knew her as few people could, and no matter what they faced each day, they were always there for each other.

It *had* been a long day, and their internal clocks were off, but still, in his arms, she slept.

And dreamed.

Angela had her own Irish great-grandmother once. A woman who told fantastic tales about the fairy people, the Tuatha dé Danaan, the old gods of Ireland, and St. Patrick, who came later, clearing the snakes from the island. Of course, according to fossil records, there hadn't been snakes in Ireland at all. As the continents shifted, the serpents would have opted for warmer climates. But the removal of *snakes* probably referred to some of the snake-like people who were in power at the time.

And still. Legend and myth.

In her dreams, Angela saw a woman. Clad in black, the long robes catching on the breeze as she lifted her hands to the heavens. She was beautiful and looked as if she sought to take the pain of others. As if she cried and keened so others need not do so.

The dream woman wasn't frightening. Somehow, she was…

Comforting. But that couldn't be right. Because the banshee came to warn that someone would die. And a comforting banshee might arrive when someone had lived almost a hundred years of life and was ready to move on.

But nothing would happen tonight. Somehow, Angela knew that.

The banshee had merely remained, ready to see them through whatever they faced. And perhaps she even waited, watching and anxious to see what might lie ahead.

* * * *

Angela was usually a person who arose in the morning fresh and ready to go in an instant. Jackson watched her for a minute when he woke.

She was staring straight up at the ceiling, awake but obviously deep in thought.

"Hey," he murmured. "You okay?"

She turned to him, grinning. "Yeah. Weird dreams about this place last night, that's all. You know, flight, time change, jumping right in."

He nodded. "Okay."

"I kept dreaming about a banshee. She was gorgeous, Jackson. Gorgeous and sweet. I mean, there are all kinds of tales about banshees not being so nice. Sometimes, the townsfolk hired *keeners* for funerals, women who lamented and cried loudly for others. They were often paid with alcohol. Then again, the banshee myth supposedly goes back to the Tuatha dé Danaan. And to the best of my knowledge, those guys weren't drinking a lot. It took human beings a while to master the creation of alcohol."

"Remember who we are," he said gently. "We don't accept anything on theory. We follow the clues and evidence."

"And get help from the dead."

"Yes, and get help from the dead," Jackson agreed with a smile. "So, we wait and see what's up. Let's get ready. I'm anxious to meet with Inspector McCray."

"And we've yet to meet the household," Angela reminded him.

"Okay. Let's do it."

Given the time change, they had luckily awakened early.

Now dressed for the day and ready, her Glock in its small holster at the base of her spine and covered by the light blue jacket she wore, Angela turned to Jackson.

"This is it. Meet the players, the household, the family. Because I believe you suspect one of them of murder."

"Well, we still don't know if there has *been* a murder," he reminded her.

Angela shrugged and nodded. "True. But—"

"If there has been a murder, yeah. Sadly, I suspect anyone close to Moira. We met the guard last night. Now, onto the rest. Breakfast with a killer." He winked. "Come on. It'll be great."

Chapter 3

Even though it was only about 7:30 a.m., Moira and her household wer already down in the kitchen when they headed downstairs to the livin quarters—the general area of the tower—with its modernized amenitie and other areas sectioned out as a dining room, a parlor, an office, and a entertainment space.

Moira was delighted to see them and introduce them to everyon They met the housekeeper, Nellie Antrim, first. As Moira had said, sh seemed to be a lovely woman in her early fifties, stout and cheerful. The they were introduced to Stewart McKenna, the steward; his wif Elizabeth; and their son, Daniel. Stewart was a fit man with a professiona look, dressed in a dark suit, his hair immaculately smoothed back, and hi eyes sharp. His wife appeared to be in her mid to late thirties, a blonde a slim and well put-together as her husband. And Daniel was like any youn boy, seemingly fascinated by them and just a little bit shy, as handsome lad as befitting the offspring of such professional and attractive parents.

"Steward," Stewart told them and grimaced. "My very name, Stewar is a derivative of the title, and the great Stewarts of history also gaine their name in such a manner. Anyway, we're delighted to have you especially amid such tragedy touching the castle. Of course, thi stronghold has been here forever. And, as you may suspect, it has bee home to many historical tragedies. Once upon a time, there were eve gallows in the courtyard. And, sorry to say, a few also lost their heads i the manor back there. But there have been great events here, too. Visit by many, and even dignitaries from foreign countries. I understand you'v been here before, Special Agent Hawkins."

Angela had continued to use her family name at work; however, in a other things, she chose to use Crow or Hawkins-Crow.

"Just Angela, please," she said lightly. "Yes, once when I was very young. I came here with my mom and dad. But seeing it as an adult, well, I'm delighted and proud that Moira has continued with her grandmother's efforts to see that it remains a family homestead and on the register as a historical holding and national treasure."

"Of course. So, how is it for an American to come to a castle?" he asked.

Jackson decided to step in. "Truthfully, *I* am fascinated. I must admit, I've never stayed in a castle before, so it is wonderful to be here. I only wish it were under better circumstances."

Stewart McKenna frowned. "But if I understand correctly, you are both with the FBI. You have no authority on foreign soil."

"We're moral support," Angela told him cheerfully. "And, of course, we're anxious to give the local inspector any help we can."

"I thought the woman died of a heart attack," Elizabeth McKenna said, looking at her husband worriedly. Like Stewart, she spoke with a charming accent.

"Any sudden death like that must be investigated," Jackson said. "Anywhere in the free world, to the best of my knowledge. We do have a crew, too. They assist Interpol and others around the world. But since Angela has a connection here, who would argue with a trip to Ireland to get to know their family better and to assist if possible?"

"Of course, of course," Stewart said.

"Aye. And it's so weird," young Daniel chimed in, grinning at them. "I love the castle. I am cool at school because I live in a haunted castle."

"And is the castle haunted?" Angela asked him.

Elizabeth laughed. "Oh, aye. Every castle in Ireland is haunted. That is how we get half of our business."

Jackson noticed her use of the word *we*. Perhaps it was natural.

Maybe she felt the castle was truly theirs, as well.

He smiled. "Any particular ghosts we should know about?" he asked.

"Let's see," Daniel told them. "There's the ghost of Edgar Woods. His name is something different in old Irish, and I only have a few words of Irish Gaelic, but…anyway, he is remembered and written up in histories and articles as Edgar Woods. He was an Irishman who rose against the Normans. He fought to regain the country, made amazing headway, and then was beheaded here right before Irish forces came in to reclaim the place. Poor dude has been hanging around for centuries."

The kid might have an accent, but he sure knew his Americanisms—

cool? Dude?

"This place is over eight-hundred years old," Elizabeth provided. "Aye. And filled with ye ghosties, 'tis! But we're thankful they've not bothered with us much."

"Then again," her husband added, "I've yet to find a wee leprechaun willing to hand over a pot of gold, and we are the Irish. Still, we've a lovely home thanks to Granny and now Moira," he said, nodding her way with a smile. "It's a sorry thing that tragedy has struck here, but I greet our friends when they bring in the tourists. And I'm afraid to say I wouldn't have recognized the poor woman had I saw her again."

"Indeed," Elizabeth said. "We were all in our chambers by then. That's what happens when one must get a child to school each day. I never saw her at all." She shrugged. "I tend to stay in the live-in tower."

"Early to bed, early to rise," Jackson said, smiling. "We have kids, too."

"Exactly," Elizabeth agreed.

"Ah, my lovies," Nellie Antrim greeted. She smiled at Jackson and Angela. "Nay, I do'na clean the entire castle, as ye may surmise. But I create a splendid breakfast if ye'd like to take a seat in the dining room."

"Breakfast would be lovely," Angela said.

"And none of that silly continental fare," Nellie said. "Irish bacon, eggs aplenty, bubble and squeak, tomatoes, soda bread, and more. Come along."

Jackson looked at Angela. She grinned and walked next to him, whispering, "Bubble and squeak are leftover fried potatoes with a touch of something else."

As they sat, she said, "Jackson has Scottish blood in him. And I believe most of us know these great breakfasts trace back to agriculture when workers were out for long hours in the fields and needed the sustenance."

"Oatmeal," Jackson said, grimacing. "It was a big staple in my family."

"The Indigenous eat a lot of oatmeal?" Elizabeth asked, seeming perplexed.

"As Angela mentioned, Mom is of Scottish descent," Jackson told her.

"Ah," Elizabeth said.

"Hearty meals, that's what's needed," Nellie said. "So, sit and enjoy, if ye please."

They sat and ate. Daniel whispered that he preferred pancakes or waffles, especially the ones with Mickey Mouse's face that he'd had when his folks took him to Disney a few years back.

The talk was general and friendly, and then Elizabeth said she had to get Daniel to school. Nellie mentioned she had arranged to meet with the cleaning crews who had been held out for the day. And Angela and Jackson were left with Moira and Stewart.

Jackson checked his watch, intrigued by the people he'd met so far but wishing he had some sense of the *real* people behind the ones they became before strangers.

Human beings, even innocent ones, often wore masks when they met newcomers. It was an instinctive self-defense mechanism. He was usually good at seeing through them, but this morning…

Nothing.

He glanced at Angela. She likely saw the question in his eyes. She shrugged in response.

"So, you're waiting on Inspector McCray?" Stewart said when the others had gone. He shook his head, glancing at Moira and then the two of them. "I'm still so confused."

Jackson studied the man. "No real confusion needed. When such a comparatively young woman dies of a heart attack in a bathroom alone, when she had no previous record of any difficulties with her heart…well, it's just one of those things that must be investigated."

"They are usually quite quick with post-mortems around here. We're out of the way a bit. I assume such things may take longer in Dublin or the big cities back in America," Stewart commented. "How's our tour entrepreneur, Mr. Mark Meadows? This must have been a first for him, giving a ghost tour and creating a ghost. Sorry, that didn't sound—"

"It's all right, Stewart," Moira assured him as she placed her hand over his. "We're all in shock over this, and I'm sure Mark is extremely upset. He instantly canceled all the tours for the rest of the week and said I should call when we felt it was time to resume."

"Are all of his tours ghost tours?" Jackson asked her.

Moira shook her head strenuously. "No. Straight history by day, and ghost tours at night a few times a week. Mark is a good man, well-educated, charming…born in the States, Irish parents, came back here for university and stayed. You'll like him."

Jackson wondered. He already had the cyber crew back home checking up on the man. What Moira had said was true. Meadows was only thirty but had managed to create his own company right out of Trinity and seemed to be doing very well for himself. And still, from the explanation of events, he had left a guest on the second floor while waiting on the first. Maybe such things were normal. But Mark Meadows was someone they would need to talk with.

Both Moira and Stewart suddenly checked their watches. Moira looked at them. "We have company."

"Your watches alert you when someone arrives, I take it?" Jackson said lightly.

"Yes. Inspector McCray is here," Moira said. "Everyone enters using the Great Tower—"

"On our way," Angela assured her, rising. "This truly was a lovely breakfast. I must thank Nellie as soon as we see her again."

Jackson and Moira got up, as well.

"It's okay," Angela assured her. "We meet a lot of law enforcement. You stay here and relax. You've been through this enough already."

Her cousin nodded and sat again, frowning but seeming happy enough to let them go.

Angela and Jackson walked down the hall to the Great Tower, where Angela hurried forward to open the door. The man they greeted seemed solid enough and quickly offered his hand to Angela and then Jackson.

"Inspector McCray," he said. "And I know you're Special Agents Hawkins and Crow from the States. We pride ourselves on Irish hospitality and agencies working well together, but you must know someone to have been granted the level of cooperation we've been ordered to give."

"We have a great benefactor," Jackson assured him. "And he is just about magical. Of course, we've not come to step on any toes. My wife is Moira's cousin."

"I know," McCray assured them and smiled. "You're welcome to anything I have. Still, by all appearances, the poor woman died of a heart attack brought on by acute arrhythmia."

"I believe it's the number of people who seem to have died by natural causes or accidents here that has Moira so upset," Jackson said.

"The old fellow in the river *was* dying of cancer," Inspector McCray said, frowning. "And he died by the castle, not inside. And the other…it was a sorry thing, but who tries to scale a wall like that?"

"That's the thing," Jackson said. "An elderly man choosing his own means of death might be one thing, but, as you said, what fool tries to scale a wall like that?"

"Sadly, the world is full of fools," McCray said. "Keeps us working," he added dryly.

"Cut and dried," Angela said. "A drowning and a crushed skull. But I am curious about the woman who just passed. How extensive was the tox screen she received?" she asked.

"Tox screen? Well, the usual, I guess. The woman didn't do drugs. She hadn't even had so much as a glass of ale or wine before the tour."

"We've asked th—" Jackson began.

"That another, more extensive post-mortem be done." McCray finished. "Aye. But why the suspicion?" he asked, then groaned. "Moira," he said. "Moira Hawkins and her banshee. Come now. You're Americans. You mustn't fall for our legends, though they are charming tales we tell our wee ones at night."

"We're here to make sure. And to be with Moira, of course," Angela said.

"And glad I am that you are. I knew her granny growing up, and a dear, dedicated—and feisty—woman she was. Well, I'll not complain. What more can I tell you?"

"We'll start with what we heard. Mark Meadows, two couples, and a teenager were still downstairs. Moira woke up and came down here to find the body in the washroom," Jackson said.

"Exactly. Which would make Moira the first person of interest if there were foul play," McCray noted. "But I know Moira to be a most generous and lovely woman. And, certainly, she has been the one to suffer for what has happened," he added quickly.

"All right," Jackson murmured. "We gave the ladies' room a quick sweep last night, but perhaps we should walk through it again, if that's all right."

Inspector McCray nodded solemnly. "Aye," he agreed.

"What about Mrs. Robertson's family?" Angela asked.

"None that we know of," McCray said. "She was a widow. Her husband was older but still died quite young a few years back. They had no children. She has a cousin she never met who lives in Canada."

"She has friends, though, I assume," Angela said.

He nodded. "Yes. We've spoken with her neighbor—a woman about her age. She was out of town the night her friend died, but she's making the funeral arrangements for when we release the body."

"You haven't agreed to do that yet?" Jackson asked.

McCray smiled. "I told you. You know someone with power. Our medical examiner has been told the body is not to be released until the two of you give the word."

They followed the inspector up the stone stairs to the second floor of

the Great Tower. Outside the ladies' room, he swept out a hand. "Go t
it, mates," he said.

They began their new search. Once again, Jackson headed to the sin
area. He had no idea what he was looking for, but he often didn't.

Evidence was never labeled at the site.

He carefully examined the restroom, bit by bit. He checked th
faucets and was ready to look for evidence on the floor.

He saw Angela was already on her knees in one of the stalls.

"May I say I'm quite grateful that even though we're in an ancien
castle, Moira and her granny saw fit to make sure the living tower wa
equipped with good showers?" he said.

He'd thought she would laugh and have some pithy reply. She didn't.

"Jackson?"

"Yeah?"

"Do you have any evidence bags?"

"I do. Why?"

"There is something here. Tiny. An extremely small square patch. I
looks like one of those used for bad backaches and the like, excep
miniature as if made for a doll."

"Coming your way."

He brought her one of the bags. She accepted it. At first, he couldn'
even see what she reached for. Then, when she used the bag to protec
the item and herself, she murmured, "It may be nothing."

"It could be something."

"I mean, there *was* a tour group here. And even with as clean as the
keep the place, there were also people here in the afternoon and the day
before."

"Again, Angela, it's all we've found. It may be something. Let's get i
to McCray."

They stepped out of the washroom.

The inspector was waiting patiently, leaning against the stone wa
with his arms crossed over his chest.

"You found something?" he asked.

"Something," Jackson said.

"We're not sure what," Angela added, producing the bag with th
tiny square.

McCray frowned. "I am impressed. You found that searching white
on-white? I had a forensic team sweeping that bathroom."

"Hey, I didn't find anything the first time either," Angela assure
him. "And—"

"It may have fallen off someone or something long before Mrs. Robertson was ever in there," McCray said. "And it might be something. I'll get it to our lab." He paused, taking a breath. "Do you want to take a quick trip to the morgue?"

Jackson and Angela glanced at each other.

"Yes, thank you," Jackson said.

"We'll take my car. I'll get you back." He gave them a weak smile. "Ms. Antrim might be making her famous Guinness chocolate mousse tonight in honor of Moira's American cousin. If that's the case, I wouldn't mind staying on a minute or so. No dereliction of duty. My job today is to make the two of you happy."

"That's fine. Thank you," Angela assured him. "Hmm. Guinness chocolate mousse? Sounds intriguing."

"You've never had it?" McCray asked.

"No, I haven't," Angela told him.

"What kind of an Irish-American are you?" He flashed her a smile.

"A mixed-up one. A total American mutt, I'm afraid," she said, laughing. "But rest assured, my Irish part is most eager to try this delicious dessert."

The drive to the morgue wasn't long. In the car, McCray pointed out some local spots of interest and asked if they would get to spend any time in Dublin.

"Probably not," Angela said. "We left quite suddenly, and Jackson—"

"Supervising Field Director for your unit, yes? And I understand you are a computer genius who can find just about anything on anyone in a matter of minutes."

Angela shrugged. "We also have two children. We're very lucky. The aunt of another of our krewe—one of our unit members—lives with us. She's wonderful with the kids. With what we do—"

"You're lucky," McCray assured her. "Ah, well, if you have time, you must explore. You think you're in a castle now? You have to see Dublin Castle and, of course, St. Patrick's Cathedral. And there's so much more. For a night spot, just about anywhere around Temple Bar."

"I've been before," Angela murmured.

"I've been, too," Jackson said. "But, yes, there are wonders we've yet to see."

"Well, then, welcome back," McCray said. "One quick stop. I'll just leave this little thing you found at the lab."

He stopped outside his headquarters and promised a quick return.

Jackson watched him as he went.

"What? You think their people can't be as good as ours?" she asked.

"I think they don't want it to be a murder," he said.

"Jackson, no American egos here. I'm willing to bet their people are great. And honest, as well. Whether they want it to be nothing or not."

"Angela," he said, "no American ego involved. I believe they'll be honest, and I'm grateful McCray is as cooperative as he is. I mean, the guy could have been a jerk."

She smiled. "No. He's a good cop—by any title."

McCray was back in minutes. "Tests to begin immediately," he assured them.

"Thank you," Jackson said.

"Trust me. We have amazing techs and equipment here. If there is something to be found, my lab people are excellent and will discover it. I promise." He let out a long sigh. "I admit, I hope it's nothing. And I'm praying this is just a sudden—and tragic—death and not murder," McCray said. "And unless there is something—"

"It will be ruled death by natural causes," Jackson finished. "Let's all hope."

McCray drove with Angela next to him. From the back seat, Jackson saw him glance at her. "It's the banshee, isn't it? Naturally, I did some research on you two. You're the head of a unit that specializes in the strange. Occult, ritual, all that."

"Yes, but we're here because Moira is a relative. I care about her," Angela assured him.

"Of course."

They signed in at the morgue, and then Doctor Byrne met them to escort them back to his autopsy room and the body.

Mrs. Robertson had been given the typical Y incision, but if not for the stitches and the presentation of the body, she might have appeared as if she were merely sleeping.

"Death occurred from natural causes from all I can discover," the doctor said.

Mrs. Robertson's shoulder-length hair was fanned out beneath her head. Jackson wasn't sure why, but he found himself studying the area behind her ear, right around her hairline.

There was something…

Just a tiny patch that seemed to be whiter than the skin around it.

A tiny, tiny space.

Like a itty-bitty transdermal patch might have been there.

"Doctor, what is this?" he asked.

The doctor frowned. "An irritation? Perhaps she was wearing something that disturbed that area of skin."

Jackson looked at Angela. She was studying the area near the woman's hairline, as well.

"Do not let the body go," Jackson said.

The door to the morgue opened, and a woman stuck her head in.

"Inspector McCray?" she said.

"Excuse me. Be right back with you," he said.

He disappeared for a minute, and Jackson and Angela continued to study the body under the doctor's watchful eye. He expressed his sorrow at such a sad death for one so young.

McCray seemed to burst back into the room, a serious frown lining his face.

"Doctor. Did you test for dart frog poisoning?" he demanded.

"What?" the doctor asked. "Sir, that is no customary test—"

"Do it." McCray turned to Angela and Jackson, staring at them with surprised confusion and distress. "That patch. Blimey. There was poison on it from a poison dart frog. Bloody hell. They come from Central and South America. How the hell? This is Ireland."

Jackson looked at Angela.

It wasn't just murder.

It might be one of the most bizarre cases they had ever encountered.

Chapter 4

"Angus. My given name is Angus," Inspector McCray said. He sat in a chair in front of the desk in Moira's office, shaking his head. Then he stared seriously at Angela. "I'll admit, I thought our high-powered politicians were just trying to play nice and keep relations between the United States of America and the Irish Republic going at full speed. To remain warm and cozy. With all due logic, why in the hell would anyone murder a random tourist in an Irish castle?"

"First, we need to find out if she was a random tourist," Angela told him.

"Right. And your people are working on it. My people are working on it. And we also know that all our intelligence experts are working on discovery. As in, how the hell did an Amazonian poison wind up in Ireland?"

"There's the catch," Jackson said. "And, as you said, our people are looking into everyone to determine if they've been in the Amazon recently. But then again, there may be partners or more involved in this. So, the question of who has been where may grow complicated. Not to mention the fact that many of the creatures can be bought in pet stores around the world."

"My people are good. I told you. They have it down to a poisonous frog from Phyllobates terribilis—the most toxic species. Do they sell those?"

"Hard to tell," Jackson said. "Supposedly, the creatures gain their toxins via their diet and then secrete it through their skin. To create something like what we found—a patch so extremely tiny and so potent—I'm thinking someone knew what they were doing."

Angela was listening to the two men while working on her computer. They were waiting for Mark Meadows to arrive. And from there, in the friendliest fashion, they would interview everyone who had been on the tour the night Mrs. Robertson was killed.

With toxin from a poison dart frog.

No wonder the banshee was wailing at such a high pitch.

"Oh, my God," Angela exclaimed suddenly.

Both men looked at her.

"I just found an article in the back pages of a New York paper," she told them, looking up. "A Professor Jared Carlson was working in a small village on the Amazon River, trying to create an antidote. Someone broke into his lab—he didn't have much security and was in the middle of nowhere, so there were no cameras. The door had a key card entry, but one of his employees admitted to having lost his. He thought he might have dropped it in the middle of the river." She licked her lips.

"I guess no one suspected that anyone would want to break into such a lab, nor were there many people in the area. Those there, of course, were anxious to see the professor succeed with his work. Medical care there is good where it exists, but villagers would have a long haul to get where any help could be found. That poison can cause arrhythmia and cardiac distress just from contact with the skin." She shook her head. "It's an oddly beautiful frog. Colorful. Apparently, the appearance warns would-be predators to stay away, but even accidentally touching the creature can be fatal."

"When was this robbery?" Jackson asked her.

"Just about three weeks ago," Angela said.

"Time enough for poison to travel around the globe," Angus McCray griped, shaking his head. "That means we must be careful coming close to anyone. And I want to suggest you speak with Moira's household and make sure everyone is aware there's a lot of poison out there. And then there are all those people who arrived for Mark Meadows' tour."

"They'll be coming in shortly. We'll begin our interviews then," Angela said.

"Of Mr. Meadows and the twenty people on the tour," Angus added. "How are we going to do this?" he asked.

"Divide and conquer," Jackson answered. "Except I think we'll all interview the last two people in the castle, those with the teenage son."

"You think one of them—?" Angus began.

"I don't think anything yet," Jackson clarified. "But they were there at the end. They would have observed Amelia Robertson last. They might have noticed a guest hanging around her. Of course, we'll talk to Mark too. Because he might have seen something."

"Right. Still…" Angus leaned forward on the desk. "Why?" he asked "She had no money. She was just a working widow. No enemies—and m people went over and over that possibility. I've worked murders before Some were domestic. Others had to do with greed. One was a bar figh gone too far. This…? Murder by poison dart frog?"

"A toxin that wouldn't have been found," Angela reminded him "without pushing the usual boundaries on tox screens at the time o autopsy."

"Right. The killer expected everyone to believe the death was natura That's even stranger. To what end?"

"Well," Jackson said lightly, "that's why we're investigators, right?"

"Aye, I'm just not accustomed to not having a clue," Angus said. H seemed to mentally square his shoulders. "But we're going to get som clues. And so help me, we will find the answer to this."

Angela glanced at Jackson. Inspector Angus McCray was provin helpful. He was far from feeling resentment, and he seemed determined.

A knock sounded on the office door.

"Yes?" Angela said.

Nellie Antrim stuck her head in. "Guinness chocolate mousse," sh announced. "I understand the castle is about to be flooded with people and ye might just be needin' some sustenance first."

"Lovely, thank you. Come on in," Angela told her.

She carried a tray with three cups of her dessert, three teacups, teapot, sugar, and cream. She set the tray on the desk, smiling but lookin like she felt a little ill.

"I'm so sorry, so very sorry." She shook her head. "Why?"

"That's what we're hoping to find out," Jackson assured her. "An thank you. This is lovely."

Angela took a spoonful of her mousse. "Delicious," she announce with a smile.

"Absolutely," Angus agreed. "I told you I was happy to come here And I believe we'll have more cooperation from our witnesses. Getting t return to a castle is better than going to an interrogation room."

Jackson wasn't eating the mousse. Angela looked at him curiously.

He shook his head. "Someone got poisoned here. Makes m suspicious of everything."

She froze, her spoon partway to her mouth.

"Couldn't be. I mean, you have been here for a bit now and…"

Angus let his thought taper off.

"Yeah. The food hasn't poisoned us," Angela reminded Jackson.

"Suspicious of all and everything," Jackson reiterated. "And—"

Another knock sounded. This time, it was Moira. Angela noted that her cousin's continual optimism and cheer seemed to be ebbing.

"Mark is here. Should I—?"

"If you don't mind that we're using your office, bring him here. Please," Jackson said.

"Mind?" Moira asked. She shook her head. "I am so very grateful."

She disappeared. A minute later, Mark Meadows walked through the door, looking around. Jackson, who had been standing behind Angela, pulled a second chair up to the desk for him.

"Thank you for coming so promptly," Jackson told him.

Angela watched the young man as he took his seat. She'd researched him and knew he had been born in the States but came to Dublin for college—and then stayed. From all appearances, at least on paper—or via computer research—he seemed to be an upright human being simply in love with history.

And legends.

"I'm sick. Just sick," he told them. "How? How could this happen? I feel like it's my fault. I mean, I couldn't go into the bathroom with the lady, but if I'd been on the second floor, I might have seen if anyone went in with her. Or after her. Or…"

His voice trailed off.

Angela decided to play good cop.

"Mr. Meadows, you can't blame yourself. The culpability lies with the person who did this. What we're hoping you can tell us is if anyone was behaving suspiciously on the tour. Did anyone try to get close to her? Try to create an instantaneous friendship, that kind of thing? Or did someone on your tour seem suspicious in any way, like not really interested in the tales you were telling?"

Mark let out a long sigh. By all appearances, he was a young, good-looking man in distress.

"I run a tour company and love to give the tours myself," he said. "But…it's a tour company. I don't deal with national secrets, banking, or flights. We don't do background checks on those in our groups. I'm trying to think, but…people chat while on a tour, especially when I'm not speaking. They talk about history, and half of them hope they'll see a ghost. I'm trying desperately to remember if anyone was close to Mrs. Robertson. She seemed like such a lovely woman. So very interested in the history of the castle. She was American but lived in Dublin and knew so much. She was a joy to talk with."

He scrubbed a hand over his face. "We all checked in at the gate, and everyone on the tour signed in—we always insist on that. You know that the gatehouse helps save the property from litigation." He offered a weak smile. "People in Ireland aren't quite as litigious as those in the States, but still. Someone getting injured on the property can be serious. The names—"

"We have all the names, thanks," Jackson told him. "But what we have is just that: a list of names. You spent time with the people on the tour."

The man nodded. "It seemed like an ordinary tour. We were just waiting for Mrs. Robertson to return from the restroom, and then Moira appeared. She went up to the washroom, and then we called emergency services, and—" He paused, glancing at Inspector McCray. "And then the inspector arrived and checked everything. We were just heartbroken that someone who seemed so lovely and young had perished up there."

"What about the couples who stayed downstairs with you?" Angela asked.

"Nice. Young couples," Meadows said. "Sherry and Max Dayton from the States, and their son, Kevin. I think he was about twelve, maybe. We warn parents there will be talk of ghosts and beheadings and...well, we don't recommend those tours for children under twelve."

"Okay. And the other couple?" Jackson asked.

"The Millers. Connie and Steve. Also American. They said they were from Georgia. They were dismayed when they had to remain until the inspector arrived. Horrified that the woman had died."

"They seemed anxious to leave," Angus said.

"I remember. Even having their kid with them, Max and Sherry seemed to understand, while Steve kept insisting his wife was about to pass out from fright, certain the castle was somehow evil." He paused, wincing. "I do tell a good ghost story," he said apologetically, then shook his head. "I've been doing tours here for four years and worked for Moira's granny before...before we lost her. I've tried in every way to keep the money flowing for Moira. She's amazing. A working actress ready to give it all up to preserve this wonderful history."

"Do you remember anyone on the tour behaving strangely in any way?" Jackson asked.

Mark shook his head, seeming at a loss. "No one seemed to be trying to get close to Mrs. Robertson. I mean, people talk to one another. Most on a tour are nice and ready to mix and mingle. And they tend to enjoy learning about those here from other countries. And, of course, they like finding out they're from the same country if that's the case. So, aye, people talked. But it was all idle chitchat, all whoever wound up being by one another wherever we were."

"Thank you," Angela told him. She glanced at Jackson. "Have we compared Mr. Meadows' list with the gatehouse's? The one signed by all the attendees?" she asked.

"I'll go get it now," Jackson said.

He left the office and headed out quickly.

Mark frowned at Angela. "Do you think they won't be the same?" he asked.

"I just think it's something we need to check. If anyone tried to get away without signing in, you might remember who it was from your list."

"Of course, of course," Meadows murmured. Then he asked, "Is Moira here?"

"She is. I'm not sure where, but yes, she's around."

He reached into his coat pocket and produced a folded sheet of paper, handing it to her across the desk.

"These are the people I accepted on the tour. Most of them paid with credit cards. Only a few paid with cash. May I…would you mind if I spoke with Moira quickly? I just want her to know I will continue to support her in any way possible when she's ready."

He spoke passionately. Angela wondered if he had a bit of a crush on her cousin.

Was it reciprocal?

He was certainly a handsome enough man. And charming. Someone who possessed a strong work ethic.

Or…

No. He wasn't related. There would be no reason for this man to want to wrest the castle from its rightful owner.

Yet…

"May I?" he pressed.

"Of course," she murmured. The second he left, she began to worry. Had she let a man with ridiculously lethal frog toxin get away? And send him right to her family?

No, no, no.

Nothing would happen now. She knew it.

The banshee isn't wailing.

* * * *

Samuel Hall from Lock-Stone Security was still standing guard at the gatehouse, manning his post, just as he was supposed to be doing.

Of course, in reality, he was *sitting* at his post. The guardhouse appeared to have all the creature comforts for those who spent hours in it.

Samuel heard Jackson coming and rose to greet him. He stepped from the gatehouse and asked anxiously, "Is everything all right?"

Jackson shrugged. "Other than a murder taking place here the night before last, everything is fine."

"Thank God," the man breathed.

"I just want to get the list of those who signed in and out of the castle for the tour the other night. And anyone else who might have visited," Jackson said.

"No one. Mark Meadows arrived early as always and waited for his guests at the entrance to the Great Tower. Mark always signs in and out. And he makes sure the others do, too. Seems to be part of his work ethic. Under normal circumstances, it would not be strange for someone to miss signing while coming in or out when a tour group is large, but Meadows is a stickler. He collects the sign-in sheets now and then, and they must align."

"That's a good thing. So, may I have that list?"

"Of course."

Sam walked back into the guardhouse and returned with a clipboard. "Just take the whole thing. You can return it when the castle is cleared for tours again."

"But we need to keep a list of anyone who comes to the castle now," Jackson told him. "I'll take all the old sheets that Meadows hasn't collected yet but leave you the clipboard. Seriously, we still need you to keep a log of everyone entering who isn't part of the household."

"Aye, sir, as you say," Sam assured him. Jackson thought he was about ready to salute but refrained from doing so.

"Thank you," Jackson told him.

"I am happy to do anything to help." Hall appeared anxious.

Jackson asked, "Are you all right?"

"Aye. I mean, I'm taking on double shifts because…"

"Because?"

Hall shook his head. "I just keep thinking if I'd been more attentive." He sighed.

"You were fine," Jackson said. "What was done would have passed through the toughest security in the world, I'm afraid, other than full body cavity searches. Don't blame yourself. Blame whoever did this."

"Right. Right. Of course. I still feel re—"

"Don't," Jackson interrupted. "Unless you were in on a conspiracy to commit murder, don't feel responsible."

"What about Moira?" he asked anxiously.

"What about her?"

"How is she?"

Jackson smiled.

"She's doing fine, honestly."

Hall nodded. "I know this sounds…silly, and maybe even wrong. I mean, I care about the poor woman who was so cruelly killed, but I don't want it falling on Moira."

"It won't."

"But—"

"She wouldn't have called us in and pressed us to discover what happened if she were involved," Jackson said flatly.

"I just don't want her to give up."

"Give up?"

"She's an actress. She's beautiful, and she has the world ahead of her. Yet she's given it all up to honor a dying woman's wishes. It was one thing for old Colleen Darien to be determined to hang on to the castle. It was all she knew. But Moira…she's seen so much of the world. She could have fawning fans wondering when her next movie might be made. She has so much promise. Yet she's here, fighting to save her family home and its history."

"You know, the time will come when she can run this place and pursue a career," Jackson assured him. "Many people do it."

"I don't know," Hall said. "Sometimes…"

"Sometimes, what?"

"Nothing, nothing."

"Sam?" Jackson persisted.

"I'd be talking out of turn."

"Talk out of turn, then. Tell me what you're thinking."

Sam looked down and then took a deep breath. He glanced at Jackson. "Aye, and all right. I just wonder sometimes…I mean, they're always professional, but…"

"But? Who are *they*, and what do you wonder?" Jackson asked firmly.

"That, um…that Mark Meadows."

"What about him?"

"I don't know. I mean, I guess he and Moira are both young an beautiful and…well, I think he has a thing for her."

"If he cares about her, he'd be the last one who would want to se her in distress," Jackson noted.

"If he cares…for her."

"You just said he did."

Again, Hall seemed to be struggling, wanting to speak.

Not wanting to speak.

"Hall, to use an Americanism, spit it out," Jackson admonished.

"Okay, okay. I just hope he cares more about her than he does th castle."

Jackson frowned. "He isn't a Darien. He has no connection to th estate. I believe Angela would be in line before Meadows. So—"

"You don't understand. The castle takes incredible management an care. Historical societies could take it over, but other than that, th expense just to purchase the property would be mammoth."

"Then there you go," Jackson said.

"Mark Meadows is a rich man. A *very* rich man. He came out c college blazing. If it came to a sale, Meadows could afford to buy."

Sam stepped back, almost as if he could deny his words by doing sc "I'm just talking. Thinking out loud. I don't know anything. Anything a all. Except it was a member of one of his tour groups who was murderec Without the tours, the woman would have never been in the castle—"

"And we're still investigating her, trying to see if someone elsewher in her life had any reason to want to see her gone," Jackson said. H smiled wearily. "Right now, well…the whole world is under suspicion."

Nodding, he turned and headed back to the castle.

He had spoken the truth. They had no real suspects yet.

Still…

Mark Meadows. The man was rich. And he knew Castle Darien a few others did. He knew all about the ghosts and possibly the *skeletons* i the closet.

The murder *had* happened on his watch.

Jackson's strides grew longer. Meadows was at the castle.

Moira was there, Angela was there.

He had a firm rule: evidence rules the way. They had none, othe than proving it had been murder. And murder most foul—and bizarre.

He was almost running when he reached the doors to the Grea Tower and streaked across the hallway to get to those within the castl and assure himself that no other evil was afoot.

Chapter 5

Jackson frowned as he came through the office door.

Angela looked at him curiously. He had just gone to retrieve the sign-in sheets. Now, she was sitting with Moira and Mark, once again speaking about the night's events.

"So, you say anyone could buy one of these creatures in a pet shop?" Mark said, sounding surprised. "But who would want a frog that can kill them if they touch it?" he asked.

"The same people who buy poisonous snakes, other reptiles, and things like tarantulas and deadly spiders," Angela said.

"Jackson," Moira said with pleasure, "I need to say again—thank you. Thank you so much for being here. I can't believe what has happened. And now… Do you think there could there be any more of that toxin around? Oh, God. I've put you at risk, too."

Jackson shook his head. "Moira, honestly, I don't believe there's more. Not at this time. And as you were all discussing, people buy the frogs as pets. They are really colorful and pretty but not something we'd want our kids to have. We think this particular strain might have come from some that were stolen from a researcher working on antidotes down in the Amazon." He gave her an assuring smile and turned to Mark. "I have the sign-in sheets."

"And I gave mine to Angela," Mark said, looking at his watch. "We've timed them coming in every fifteen minutes."

"Where's the inspector?" Jackson asked Angela.

"Downstairs. He brought the tray to the kitchen. He'll be right back," Angela told him as she accepted the list he handed to her.

She quickly looked over the pages and then back at the group waiting for her to speak again.

"The lists match," she said.

"Then it was someone who came in the tour group," Mark said, his voice low and weary.

"Improbable but not impossible," Jackson said. "Still, we need to start interviewing people, and it's best if we do so alone."

"Of course," Moira agreed, rising.

"I'm taking the dining room," Angus told her when he returned.

"Right. Fine," Moira acknowledged. "And—"

"We have the final two couples who were here that night coming in last. We'll meet them all in the dining room," Angela said, nodding. "For now, I'm keeping the office—"

"And I'm heading for the entertainment room," Jackson said.

"Yeah, great entertainment," Angus said dryly.

Jackson looked at him, arching a brow. "Sorry," he said. "I'm just... I'm still having trouble believing all this." He was quiet for a minute. "And the thought that the killer might have easily gotten away with it if you two hadn't believed Moira and used your powerful friend to get here."

"Inspector, you have been a team player since we arrived," Jackson told him. "We thank you."

Angus nodded. "Well, then, Moira—"

"Mark and I will head out to the courtyard. He can tell me some more tales about my home," Moira provided.

"You know all the tales," Mark said.

"Not the way you tell them," she replied with a shy smile.

Angela knew, then. Mark cared about Moira. And it was mutual. They were a handsome couple, just like Barbie and Ken.

Unless...

No. Nothing would happen. Not when they were all there and knew the two of them would be together. But with a killer cunning enough to almost get away with murder by making use of a tiny tab filled with poison dart frog toxin...

The others left Angela alone in the office. She began her third of the first fifteen interviews.

No one stood out. Everyone was horrified, and most were scared. They all wanted to go back home.

A woman had been murdered. And a murderer was still at large—a cunning one who could kill with subterfuge and a smile.

It was easy to understand their fear. Yet even as Angela met her five guests from the night of Mrs. Robertson's death, she wondered if one of them might have been part of a conspiracy, one in which someone from somewhere had delivered the toxin for a resident of the very tower they were staying in.

* * * *

"Anything?" Angus asked Jackson as the last of the first fifteen visitors left the castle, and Jackson joined the inspector in the dining room.

"Nothing concrete. I had one Parisian, two Americans, and two young women from Dublin. I looked for tells, the things we've been trained to seek out to know when people are lying, and didn't see anything."

"And still," Angus said, "you're suspicious of everyone, just like me."

"Well, *someone* brought that toxin in here," Jackson said.

Angus nodded dully. "Do you really think…?"

"That it's gone from the castle? I do. Because we were never supposed to realize the woman had been murdered."

"And wouldn't have—"

"Don't. Don't do that to yourself," Jackson said. "We got to the truth, and we couldn't have made a move without your cooperation. You've been great to work with. Accept the wins, please. We have to move on."

"At least now we know. Unfortunately, the press somehow got ahold of the information immediately. I just hope…" The inspector trailed off and blew out a breath.

Jackson cocked his head.

"What?"

"I think the castle is supposed to appear cursed, not haunted. A drowning? A fall? A heart attack—but one proven to have been caused by a toxin."

"Hmm," Angus said.

Jackson knew Angus would likely remain aggravated with himself—as would he in the man's shoes. But he also knew Inspector McCray was fully with them now, and he was equally determined to uncover the truth.

Angela joined them, making a face. They didn't have to ask her if she'd met anyone suspicious. She would have immediately said something.

"What now?" she asked, taking a seat.

"Moira and Mark have seen the others out. They'll bring in the last two couples and the kid, though I'm not sure we should be questioning a child," Angus advised.

"He might have seen something," Jackson said simply. "Who's first?"

"Connie and Steve Miller from Augusta, Georgia," Angela said. "Connie is a geography professor at a local college and originally from Kentucky. Steve is a medical doctor and moved from North Dakota. They met on a dating app while on vacation in the Caribbean, and it was love and new jobs all around about two and a half years ago."

"Americans," Angus pointed out.

"With no relationship whatsoever to Castle Darien," Angela reminded them.

She fell silent as the couple entered the dining room. They were young—just in their late twenties according to the research she had done on them. Due to their extensive social media accounts, she also knew what they'd been up to these last years.

Everyone in the room rose to greet them.

Steve immediately set an arm around his wife's shoulders and admitted, "We're terrified just to be here now. We heard what happened. Please, don't touch us."

Angela nodded solemnly. "Not to worry, Dr. Miller. We have no intention of touching you. But we are talking to everyone, desperately hoping one of you might have seen something. In fact, *did* you see anyone touch Mrs. Robertson or perhaps head into the ladies' room before or after her?"

A petite brunette, Connie Miller looked at her husband and shook her head. Then she looked at Angela. "I mean, there were instances when we brushed by each other in the hallways or while moving. Mrs. Robertson was next to me on the stairs when we first went up to the second floor, but I swear we didn't do this. You can search our hotel room. You can search me… I didn't do this. Please, we'd have no reason."

"We're not suggesting you did." Jackson turned to Dr. Miller. "Did you see anyone close to Mrs. Robertson?" he asked.

Steve started to shake his head but then frowned. "Yeah, actually. The tour guide. The master of history himself. You know, I think he's one big phony. He grew up in the United States, and now he feigns that Irish accent when he's telling stories. He had his arm around the now-dead woman when we first arrived. Oh, my God. He did it. Mark Meadows did it."

Inspector McCray gave the man an icy stare. "We don't throw accusations around without facts. So, please, I would appreciate it if you didn't make assumptions."

"She ruffled the kid's hair," Connie Miller said suddenly.

"What?" Jackson asked. "You mean Mrs. Robertson? Which kid? The remaining couple's son? Kevin?"

"Yeah, yeah, I think that was his name," Connie Miller said, nodding. "She was…well, she seemed to be very nice. Some of us weren't too crazy about a kid being on the tour. We thought the guide might water it down a bit, but Mrs. Robertson liked him from the start. She took his hand now and then and chatted with his parents. They were very friendly."

Steve Miller stood. "We can't tell you anything more. So help me, if we knew anything, we'd tell you. It's horrible. And was bad enough to think the poor woman had a heart attack, but now, after hearing what has been on the news all day, and knowing what really happened…"

Angela looked at McCray, as did Jackson. The inspector just shook his head. He didn't know any more than they did about who had given the information to the media.

"Anyway, we're leaving. We're getting out of here—"

"Sorry to say, you're not, sir," Inspector McCray said. "You'll stay in case we need you again."

"You can't do that. We're American citizens—"

"I *can* do that. Don't worry. We'll have people guarding you at your hotel. But until this matter is resolved, I'm afraid everyone on the tour that night will be enjoying Irish hospitality."

Steve Miller set his arm around his wife again, angrily turning and leaving the room without another word.

"Can you really keep them here?" Angela asked him.

He grinned. "I'm not sure if I could without help. But it seems your great American benefactor can make just about anything happen."

"Kudos to Adam," Jackson murmured.

Then Moira politely ushered the last family into the room, Sherry and Max Dayton, and their son, Kevin. She made introductions all around.

The boy was cute. He reminded Angela of Corby. They were close in age, too. Kevin appeared to be worried but not frightened.

"Hey," Angela said gently, addressing the teen. "Kevin, I'm so sorry you had to come here—"

"It's all right," the boy said, the words coming out in tandem with his father's.

Kevin grinned, but it quickly faded. "She was nice. The lady. She was so nice. We want to help if someone hurt her."

The three of them sat, and Jackson asked them if they had seen

anyone especially close with Mrs. Robertson or anything that might hav
appeared at all suspicious.

"This is so hard," Sherry Dayton said. "I mean, we were visiting wit
each other. It was one of the best tours we'd been on. Mr. Meadows is s
very good. He changes voices and everything when speaking about event
from the distant past. And he knows so much. I thought I knew Iris
history, but my knowledge is nothing to the way he knows it. He tell
facts first—just the truth of the events. And then explains what has bee
reported as being *seen* since. And the group…well, everyone seemed s
very nice. We all chatted between stories and…"

Her voice trailed away with a whisper of misery.

"I can say the same and little more, I'm afraid," Max Dayton tol
them. "She was kind. She seemed to love kids. Actually, she told us sh
loved kids and approached Kevin right away. She said he was amazing, s
interested in history that wasn't even his. It was so cute. She told him t
look out for leprechauns while he was here. Said they could be trickster
but weren't mean—they just liked to play harmless pranks. Kevin wa
with her, holding her hand for most of the tour."

Angela hated to do it, but she turned her attention back to Kevir
"So. She was really, really nice, huh?"

"Oh, yeah," Kevin said. "And almost as good as the tour guy. Sh
was fun. And she didn't act like she had something icky stuck to her foo
when she was around me. Not like some other people. I didn't even min
her holding my hand, even though I'm too old for that."

"Others acted that way to you?" Angela asked.

"The, um, the couple who just left," Max said, replying for his son. "
heard them. They asked the guide why kids were allowed on a ghost tou
They said kids should be in bed, not out that late at night."

"Connie and Steve Miller?" Jackson asked.

"I didn't really catch their names," Max said. "But we saw then
leaving as we arrived tonight. I was going to wave or do something, bu
they acted like they didn't see us."

"It's clear they don't like kids," Sherry said. "But I didn't see them d
anything. Kevin seemed to be near Mrs. Robertson most of the time, an
they didn't want to be near Kevin. Well, I think maybe on the stairs
Those old stone stairs are dangerous if you don't pay attention. We wer
all close. Maybe the woman was close to Mrs. Robertson then. I don
really know."

"I do," Kevin said.

Angela turned to the boy. "You know what, Kevin? Please, tell me," she urged.

"I know that lady was right next to Mrs. Robertson on the stairs. I know because, well, I'm a kid, and we're better at some stuff than adults. I tried to stay behind her, just in case she slipped."

"Kevin," his mother admonished, "if anyone had fallen, you're not big enough or—"

"Mom, chill. Please," Kevin said, rolling his eyes.

He leaned forward, talking to Angela earnestly. "This isn't just because that lady was mean to me. Honest. She was right next to Mrs. Robertson. And I swear, at one point, she had her hand on Mrs. Robertson's shoulder. I saw it. I swear to you… I'd swear on a stack of Bibles."

"We go to church—" his mother began.

"I'd swear it right in the middle of St. Patrick's Cathedral," Kevin continued.

"Thank you, Kevin," Angela told him. "We will check it all out. We know you're not lying. She told us herself that she was next to Mrs. Robertson on the stairs."

"Do any of you know anything else?" Angus asked, looking from one of them to the other. He frowned suddenly and then added, "Wasn't it strange to you that the three of you and Dr. and Professor Miller were left downstairs with Mark Meadows while Mrs. Robertson was upstairs, and the others on the tour had left?"

"Honestly? I didn't want to stay," Sherry said. "I didn't want to be near them anymore, in any way. I mean, we understand. We have friends who don't have children, and they don't know how to deal with them or accept them. But Kevin is a good kid. He's quiet. He listens. He wasn't bothering anyone on the tour, and they were the only two who seemed…almost hostile."

She reached out and fixed her son's hair, much to his embarrassment. "But Kevin was so into the stories. He wanted to ask more about the Vikings and what had been going on here when the Irish gained a hold against them. This castle was built during the Norman age, but Mr. Meadows made mention of the Vikings, and Kevin loves all things Viking and wanted to ask more questions. So…we stayed."

"And then stayed more when the inspector came," Max said, nodding toward Angus.

"I didn't mean to bug Mr. Meadows," Kevin suddenly chimed in. "But he told us we could ask him questions about anything."

"I'm sure he meant that and appreciated all your interest," Angela told the boy.

"And *we* appreciate that you understood the severity of the situation, waited for clearance from me, and came back in today," Angus told the group.

Angela turned to Kevin again. "Did you see anyone else near Mrs. Robertson, anyone who might have hugged her? Touched her?"

Kevin shook his head.

"I heard she was close to Mark," Jackson prompted.

"I don't know how or when. Most of us were already here when Mrs. Robertson arrived. She was almost one of the last people, just making it, and only about five minutes before we were set to begin," Sherry said.

"I see," Angela murmured. "Well, then—"

Max and Sherry rose, and Kevin immediately followed suit.

"It's okay. You don't need to give us the spiel. We have no intention of leaving Ireland until…well, until you say we're free to go," Max said. He laid a card on the table. "This is where we're staying, my cell phone, and Sherry's number. We're here if you need us. Of course, if you *do* learn anything… The woman was kind. So kind."

"Of course," Angela said. "And thank you so much."

They exited the dining room. Moira had been waiting just behind the dividing wall and thanked them sincerely, too, smiling at Kevin as they all walked out.

Left together, Angela, Jackson, and Angus stared at one another.

"Why in the hell would a couple of Americans want to kill Mrs. Robertson? I mean, we can't just believe it was the Millers because they seem to be rather nasty people, but…"

"They lied," Angela said flatly. "They lied about Mark hugging Mrs. Robertson, something no one else mentioned in any way, shape, or form."

"So we have suspects," Jackson said, looking at the others. "Now how the hell do we prove they did it? Angela, can you—?"

"I'll find out if they've ordered any poisonous pets. That is if they ordered any and left a *record*, but I doubt that will be the case."

Angus shook his head. "There has to be something. It's bizarre to think an American couple came to Ireland to murder a stranger."

"More than bizarre," Angela agreed. "There must be a relationship somewhere, a connection. If they're guilty. Just touching someone in a non-aggressive or non-sexual manner isn't illegal."

"So," McCray mused, "just what could the relationship be?" He looked at them before adding, "And just how many people might be involved in one way or another?"

"*And*," Angela provided, "to what end? If we knew that, maybe we could piece this together."

"Someone wants the castle," Jackson said flatly.

"But, Jackson," Angela murmured, "I told you—"

"We definitely need to look into the Millers' finances," Jackson said. "Though I don't know what they'd want with an Irish castle."

"Hey," Angus protested. "Wouldn't *anyone* want an Irish castle?"

Jackson grinned, but it quickly faded. "Wait. *Doctor* Miller. The man would know that just a brush with poison dart frog toxin could cause serious damage or death," he pointed out.

"And his wife teaches geography," Angela said.

"They do make good suspects," Jackson agreed. "Now, we just need the thing that's necessary in both our countries." He looked at Angela and then Angus.

"It would be nice to know the motive," Angus said.

"It would, indeed," Jackson agreed. "But what we need is—"

"Proof," Angela said softly. "And here's the thing. If we can get something that resembles proof against them, they could be coerced into telling us who else is involved, if anyone is. Therein, we just might find the motive."

Chapter 6

With the others gone, Jackson excused himself for a minute to call Bruce McFadden, giving him a list of the information they needed. Bruce reminded him that Angela was customarily their information guru, but then he laughed and assured him it was an intriguing case, and they were on it.

"Financials are important," Jackson reminded him. "And searches for any of these people who might have purchased a poison dart frog for a pet, or—because of that lab robbery in South America—anyone who might have traveled along the Amazon."

When he returned to the office, Angus and Angela were talking about the interviews they'd conducted, shaking their heads. They suggested again that it seemed—at the very least—that Connie and Steve Miller were under suspicion.

Angela glanced at him, and he nodded.

Angus laughed out loud. "I don't need to worry. You have the innumerable machinations of the FBI gathering the information we need on our guests. But our people are working, too."

Jackson nodded at him. "And that's great because night has come on. We have night crews, of course, but if *your* machine is whirring—"

"They'll get what we need," Angus assured him. "Mr. Meadows is still at the castle. And Moira hasn't returned here."

"Let's find them," Angela said.

And they did.

Mark was in the kitchen, chatting with Nellie about Irish food.

When they all filed into the room, he looked at them expectantly—and hopefully.

"Anything?" he asked.

"Nothing solid, no. Oh, except that Kevin is one good kid," Jackson said easily.

None of them knew who had leaked everything about the murder at the castle to the press, but they were in silent agreement that no one else would get any information from them until the situation had been resolved.

"He is a good kid," Mark said.

"Dinner will be ready in about an hour," Nellie told them. "And forgive me if we're not all spic and span. I've not had the cleaning crew in, being as, well, we're not having others in at this time."

"Of course. No worries," Angela said. "And the castle is evidently loved and cared for. Trust me, none of us could clean a whole castle on our own. We're grateful you're such a wonderful cook."

The woman smiled. "Ah, well, I worked for Colleen for decades, long before our dear Moira returned from the States. And here she is. Moira, where—?"

"Making sure our visitors were safely out," Moira said.

"I was telling these lovelies about Colleen and my cooking expertise. She loved for me to experiment with food, adored the classics and all that came our way from afar—especially empanadas," she said cheerfully.

"Nellie makes one hell of an empanada," Moira said.

"Empanadas. Great," Jackson murmured and looked at Angela.

She looked back at him with a slightly apologetic smile. She was about to do something he might not like.

"Mark?" Angela said. "Would you be willing to take us on one of your ghost tours? I can't help but think it might help us if we knew more about what was going on that night."

"Angela—" Moira began.

"No, no, Moira. It's fine," Mark said enthusiastically. "I love my tours. Come on, we'll start over in the Great Tower." Moira got up and walked out with him.

Jackson held back, catching Angela's arm lightly and whispering, "Ghost tour? What if we see a ghost?"

"That's just it, Jackson. We've been here, in a castle that's likely seen more bloodshed than can be imagined, and haven't seen even one ghost," she told him.

"Maybe those who died are happy with their final outcome. It *is* now the Republic of Ireland," Jackson reminded her.

"True," she said softly. "I just hoped that…well, I hoped maybe

Colleen Darien stuck around after she died."

"But she was happy, too. Her beloved granddaughter was home ready to take the reins of the castle and bring it safely into the twenty-firs century," Jackson reminded her.

"Still, why is this a ghostless castle?" Angela said.

"Hey. We're doing the tour. We'll see what we see, and hear wha may be of interest later," Jackson assured her. "Come on. We don't wan to look like we're whispering about these guys."

Mark gave an excellent tour. He started back—way back—tellin them that the first instances of human beings was approximately thirty three thousand years ago, with more evidence showing that Homo sapien were populating the area by 10,500 BC to 7,000 BC. As the ice recede about that time, Ireland's prehistoric era began, bringing in new evolutio and populations. He then moved forward to more of what they bot knew already, the history of the Gaels, Vikings, and Norse, and the onward to the British royalty, who would eventually claim the island.

"I believe you know about St. Patrick. He was brought here first as young enslaved person, then returned as an adult. And, as you know, h might not have gotten the nonexistent snakes out of Ireland, but he di create a country of Christians. Sadly, religion was the cause of endles wars to come throughout the century as British royalty laid claim agai and again, and revolts broke out. So, in the Great Tower, we have th ghost of Shamus, an Irish king brought low by the Normans. And in th courtyard, we have the ghost of one of the first of the family to call th castle home, Lady Siobhan Darien. She was hanged for what the invadin English called treason, but she swore there was none when she merel fought for her own land on Irish soil."

They traveled through much of the castle as Mark spoke, and as h told them more about Siobhan Darien, Jackson smiled.

He figured he was right. Those who had died were able to move o because this was now the Republic of Ireland.

"So many wars over religion," Moira murmured.

Jackson was about to answer, but Mark did instead, shaking his heac "I'm sure religion was often given as an excuse, but you have t remember, the Catholic landowners were stripped of their property which was then handed over to the Protestant followers of whoever wa the English ruler at the time. We've seen it all over the world. Ideologie scare people and…seriously." He grinned at Jackson and Angela. "I grev up in the States. I know why the Founding Fathers wanted to guarante freedom of religion—which meant freedom for all religions, not just one" own. They watched people use religion—you know, the devil turning women into witches—to further their agendas. Some were terrified, those who believed the darkness of the endless woods might well hold evils. But I still say that when people blame religion, there's a deeper cause most of the time."

"Well said," Jackson told him. "We can see why you're such a beloved guide."

The man blushed, and Jackson smiled. Angela was giving him a nod of approval for his comment."Well, look, it's dinner time," Moira said.

As they turned to go back to the Darien Tower, Jackson put his hand on Angela's arm to pull her closer to him before whispering, "See? No ghosts. They're happy now. The northern part of the island was populated by those who chose to stay British, and the south is now the Republic of Ireland. Our ghosts are all happy."

She smiled and nodded. "Nothing like a happy ghost. Still. Cool castle, huh?"

"Very cool castle," he agreed. "And even cooler after dinner." They headed to the dining room. Nellie was already setting covered food platters on the table.

It had been set for all of them, including Mark and Angus.

"You didn't have to have me here for supper," Mark said.

"Nor me," the inspector added.

"We're delighted to have you both," Moira assured them. "Nellie loves to cook for a crowd. I feel bad when it's just Stewart, his family, and me. Nellie should have a restaurant or a pub so she can cook for dozens of people every night."

They sat down and were soon joined by Stewart, Elizabeth, and Daniel. Again, the teen reminded Jackson of his son, Corby. Like Corby, Daniel had learned manners and how to be polite, yet still be a normal and energetic boy.

Naturally, Stewart looked from Angus to Jackson and Angela. "Anything?" he asked quietly.

"We just keep moving forward. This is one tangled web," Angus told him. "So, what was up with the family McKenna today?"

"Rugby," Daniel announced. "And my team won."

"Daniel was the star of the show today," Elizabeth said.

They talked about the game and the food. They discussed anything but the murder that had taken place at the castle.

When they were nearing the end of the meal, Nellie ran in to tell them she'd be right back. She wasn't sure who was on duty, but she wanted to run a meal down to the gatehouse.

"That's great, Nellie," Moira said. "But you've worked all day. We're all capable of picking up after such a lovely supper. Let us run down to the gatehouse and clean up for—"

"Nay, lass, nay," Nellie protested. "You people just relax. I enjoy feeding the lads at the gatehouse. I'll be right back, and I know how to do the pickin' up meself."

As soon as she was gone, Moira and Angela looked at each other. "Hell, yes, let's do it," Angela said. The two were up in a flash, sweeping serving dishes off the table. Jackson quickly got to his feet, as did the others, including Daniel.

They were an odd team, but a good one. In minutes, they had the table cleared. Moira loaded the dishwasher while Jackson and Angela rinsed the dishes. Stewart and Elizabeth wrapped and put away some of the leftover food with Daniel at their side, ready to gather what they needed and move things around in the refrigerator.

Even Mark seemed to fall right into a pattern as he listened to anything Moira said, ready to switch from place to place to help. When Nellie returned, she was stunned.

"Aw, lovies. How sweet and kind. And unnecessary. 'Tis me job. But you are dear people, and I am grateful to you and ready for me bed."

"And we need to leave so you all can get some sleep," Angus said, looking at Mark.

"Aye. Right. Time to leave," Meadows agreed. Then he turned to Moira. "I…just. Other people work for me and can handle things when I'm gone. I will be here anytime, day or night, if you need me."

"Thank you, Mark," Moira whispered.

He nodded.

"I'll be here bright and early in the morning," Angus said more matter-of-factly. "Of course, you can call me at any time, too."

"Will do," Jackson assured him.

The two left, and Elizabeth yawned. "I'm to bed."

"We're all to bed," Stewart agreed.

"I could play a few video games," Daniel said.

"I'm sure you could," his father told him. "But, we're to bed. And, as always, Moira, we're here if you need us. Hopefully, we're out of the way when you don't."

She hugged him, then squeezed Elizabeth and Daniel, making the boy blush.

They headed to their bedrooms.

Moira sighed.

"Ye sweeties cleaned me kitchen. Yah. I'm also to bed," Nellie said.

"We'll walk together," Angela told Moira.

She smiled. They all headed upstairs, and Angela and Jackson watched Moira enter her bedroom and waited until they heard the door lock.

It did.

They moved into their room, where Jackson immediately pulled his wife into his arms.

She laughed, happy to be there. "Well, we can't use the castle as an excuse anymore," she teased. "I mean, you know...been there, done that."

"I've been there time and again. And still..." He nuzzled her neck.

She laughed. It was an amazing way to shake off the day. Of course, showers were good first. Such sweet foreplay could be afforded in a shower, though they quickly found the bed once things got too slippery.

When Jackson finally slept that night, he felt strangely at peace.

Despite the odd murder they were so desperately trying to solve.

But they had suspects. Now, they just needed a few facts and the proof that was known as evidence.

* * * *

Angela heard it. A sound so soft in the night it almost wasn't there...

It could have been the memory of a song, replaying in her subconscious mind, something on the whisper of a night breeze.

But it wasn't.

She opened her eyes. Jackson slept peacefully at her side. She hesitated. He was a man who heard the slightest rustle, the smallest nuance of movement.

No one moved in the room. Yet she still heard the sound. It seemed to be coming from the courtyard.

But they had tried to find ghosts in the castle. If any resided here, they didn't care to make an appearance. She wasn't sure Jackson believed in the concept of the banshee.

But he believed in her. She knew it. And still...

She wondered if she could possibly slip from the room, go down to the hall, and then get out into the courtyard for a look.

As silently as possible, she slid from the bed, remembering when Victoria had been just a baby and she'd tried to tend to her at night without waking her husband. Jackson was a great dad. He'd been happy to handle any nighttime situations with Corby or Victoria. And while he was capable of most things, he couldn't breastfeed. And while she'd worked from home in those early months, he had gone into the office. The Krewe of Hunters had a lot of perks, but they were a special unit. He took his job seriously—as they all did. But as field supervisor, he was determined to never fail their founder and great benefactor.

She made it out of their bed and quickly pulled on one of her long, white cotton gowns, warm enough for a bit of a walk through the castle.

She kept an eye on him. So far, he hadn't moved. His eyes remained closed. His arm had been around her but now rested on the bed.

She hurried to the door and quietly went out into the hall.

Low, subtle lights lit the tower lest anyone need something—water or anything else—in the darkness of the night. It was easy for Angela to quicky run down the old stairs, through the hall, and to the small arched doorway that led out to the great courtyard.

And there she was. Dead center of the courtyard, where, so they had been told, the gallows had once stood. Now, there was just a large dais surrounded by beautiful flowering shrubs and small trees.

She stood there, looking at the Great Tower, dressed in flowing black from her hooded cape to her toes.

She was beautiful. Her hair was nearly as dark as her garment; her features perfectly aligned, eyes wide, and lips generous. And as Angela watched, she let out a soft moan like what had penetrated Angela's mind, even as she slept.

Angela approached her slowly, and as she neared the dais, the banshee turned and looked at her. The low moan turned to silence as she stared at Angela in surprise and consternation.

"You see me," she whispered.

"I do," Angela said.

"And you're…alive."

"I believe so." Angela smiled.

"Then you must help me. You *must* help me," the banshee whispered desperately.

* * * *

Jackson had heard Angela moving around the room and assumed she was just restless or seeking something for the morning. He didn't open his eyes but rather waited for her to lie back down beside him so he could slip an arm around her and pull her close to drift back to sleep.

But she didn't slide back into bed. Instead, she quietly opened the door and slipped out of the room.

He jumped up, found a pair of jeans to wear, and then threw on a shirt without bothering to do up the buttons. He slipped into his shoes and headed out of the room.

She wasn't in the hallway, so he hurried down to the kitchen, the dining room, and the office. There was no sign of her.

She was a capable agent, well-schooled in self-defense. He knew that. He also knew he loved her desperately, and they were at their best when working as a team.

But she was nowhere in the castle's living areas.

Then it occurred to him that she might have slipped out to the courtyard, where they had thought they might meet up with a ghost.

He burst outside.

And there she was, standing before the dais.

And atop the platform…

Was a woman, ethereal and beautiful, clad in flowing black that almost seemed to be a part of the night.

The woman looked at him. Alarm crossed her features before she flickered as if she might quickly shimmer away into nothing.

"It's all right. Please," Angela begged the being. "Please, he's with me. My husband. He sees you, too. And if anyone can help, believe me, it's Jackson."

The image became clearer.

Chapter 7

Angela anxiously watched the banshee and hoped she wouldn't disappea because of Jackson's arrival. Regardless, she could never be angry wit him.

He had come because he would always have her back. The fact tha he had followed her made her smile. It underscored his determination t not only be the best damned partner professionally but also the greates life partner.

The banshee chose not to disappear. Jackson moved forward, joinin Angela. They stood at the dais below the banshee, and Angela asked he softly, "What is going on here?"

"I don't know!" the banshee wailed softly, a slight Irish lilt to he words. "I…came when I knew Colleen's time was coming. It was righ Her life had been beautiful, full of care and service for and to others. took her gently home, trying to let Moira know that her grandmother wa loved. She…Moira is a special woman, gifted. And I was here for her. Bu then…"

The banshee paused, seeming distressed.

"We don't know everything," she whispered. "We sense much… felt the heartache of the elderly gentleman who drowned, and I…I kne his fear. I felt a shuddering thud when the man fell to his death. This tim I knew a woman was in distress and felt an evil presence entering th castle. I tried to warn the others, but only Moira could hear me. An when she came, it was too late. But I knew it wasn't right. We sens things, as I said, and I knew…I *knew* evil had entered the castle."

"Do you know who is bringing it in?" Jackson asked.

The banshee shook her head.

"It's a bit like watching smoke disperse. Sometimes, it blows away. Other times, it remains. Locked in. This…I still feel it. I have the sense that it lingers. Not strong at the moment, the greatest amount seemed to sweep away that night, but a hint of it is still here as if it could summon a greater darkness."

"We may have discovered something. People who came here and brought part of that darkness with them. But do you know why? Why would someone want to kill anyone here?" Jackson asked. He glanced at Angela and continued with, "Angela and I can speak with the dead when they remain and wish to reach out to the living. Yet here we are in this ancient castle, and we haven't been able to see or reach anyone from the past."

"Because they can rest. Because I helped them move on," the banshee said softly. "I am the only ghost here, and I remain for the others. The lady who died…she was stunned, shocked, and her soul was in pain. So, I brought her onward as quickly as possible so she could find some peace. But you say you may have found those responsible for the darkness? They don't deserve to die. Instead, they should pay for what they're doing to those innocent of evil. Those who care for others."

"We are doing our best to find the people responsible for this evil," Angela told her.

"You've been around for years, I imagine," Jackson said gently. "And I believe you know how years roll forward, how things must be done, and…"

"You need proof," the banshee said softly.

"We do. And we are working on it, I promise," Angela assured. "If you'll allow us, we'll bring you everything we discover. And—"

"You need my help," the banshee said passionately. "Listen, and I will warn you. I feel evil when it's about to strike. I feel it, and if you heed my call, I can help."

"We will listen," Jackson vowed. He glanced at Angela and told the banshee, "My wife hears you more clearly than I can, but we are together in this, and we will come when you call."

The banshee nodded.

"If you please," Angela said softly. "How… I mean, as a child, I was taught that a banshee came to warn of death and was a ghost herself, a lamenter for those who needed help to understand loss and grief."

"You ask if I am really a ghost?" the banshee asked. "Indeed. As I said, I am. Here by choice, to warn, yes, but also to help others. My name is Lady Doreen Darien. I was killed in 1565 after the Acts of Supremacy and Uniformity were passed. My husband resisted, and they came after him. I ended up between him and an arrow, and…we both perished. When I'm not here, I'm with him, and we are grateful to learn there is a time and place for all where hatred has ceased, and forgiveness reigns. But as for what is happening here…there is a time and place for that, too. And more innocents may well be taken before their time."

"We will work together," Jackson told her.

"I am ever watchful," she vowed.

"Thank you again," Angela whispered, and Jackson nodded.

The banshee disappeared.

"Lady Doreen Darien," Angela murmured.

"She must have been a beautiful human being," Jackson said, "A truly beautiful person. She didn't say so, but I imagine the kindest souls are chosen for this, even if some think of the banshee's cry as nothing more than an evil warning that death is on the way. But speaking of all of this, we need to get some sleep. Even with her help, our days will only grow longer and harder before this ends."

Angela nodded, then looked at him and smiled. "She's real. And she's beautiful, isn't she?"

"Absolutely," he said, slipping an arm around her as they headed for the door that led back to the hall. "If she's real, what do you think about leprechauns?"

"I don't know. I haven't seen any. The idea is that if you can catch one, they might try to escape you by giving you their pot of gold."

"That would be nice."

"Would it?" Angela asked. "How would it change our lives? Would we quit and just go off and do whatever we wanted? No, right? We live the lives we chose, kind of like…"

"Like the banshee choosing her role," Jackson finished.

"Kind of, yeah."

He nodded. "A pot of gold wouldn't change anything. Except we wouldn't have to worry about college funds for the kids."

Angela laughed softly. "We already have accounts set up for them that we add to regularly. And if something ever happens to us, Adam will see to the kids. So, hmm…a pot of gold. Vacations in Hawaii? Traveling?"

"Well, we're in a castle in Ireland. We travel," he reminded her with a grin.

"Yeah, but when this one is over, maybe we'll let the McFadden brothers keep control of the office for a bit longer and take a week in Hawaii. What do you think? Not that I don't love Ireland, but the castle doesn't come with a beach."

"Hmm," Jackson murmured. "Maybe. That way, we can have the best of the old and new worlds. We'll see. Right now, let's go see about our delightfully comfortable pillows."

Angela nodded, happy to lean against him as they returned to their room and curled up together for the remainder of the night.

* * * *

They received the call from Bruce before they left their room the following morning.

"Well, we searched credit card records and came up with nothing. We can't find anything anywhere that indicates any of the people on your list might have purchased a poison dart frog from a pet store somewhere."

"Thanks, Bruce," Jackson said. He had the phone on speaker so he and Angela could both listen. "I never thought our person, determined enough to manage a lethal, doll-sized transdermal patch, would have used a credit card to buy the frog. They would have likely used cash so they left no paper trail."

"Right. But we aren't giving up. We found residences for all our people, and we're checking security and traffic cams to see if we can find anyone going into a pet store. With special attention, of course, given to the Miller couple," Bruce told them.

"He's a doctor," Angela said. "And she teaches geography at the college level. That makes me think if we happen to be on the right trail, she'd know about the research being done in the Amazon, and he would know what is needed to kill someone."

"You trained us well. We're also following up on passports—"

"Neither of them will have been down to the Amazon themselves," Angela said. "I think we need to check into Professor Miller's students."

"We're on that, too. Like I said, you trained us well."

Angela smiled at Jackson. "Thanks," she said quietly to Bruce.

"Of course. We're doing every bit of research humanly possible. I've even got artificial intelligence working on some of this, except A.I. doesn't have instinct or gut reaction. From the information you provided, we are working on the theory that the Miller couple killed Mrs. Robertson. Now, we need proof, or at the very least, additional clues for you to investigate. Why, though? The motive's the kicker. I can't figure it out."

"Yeah, we're working on that here, too. The theory is that someone wants Moira out of the picture. But again, the question remains. Why.

Anyone trying to stake a claim to the castle would be in a battle for years. Even with as distant as she is," Jackson said, "Angela would be in the running to inherit the place. Naturally, historical societies would love to take it over, but that wouldn't benefit anyone with a massive cash flow or anything of the sort. Moira is doing all the right things to stay afloat and keep the castle as historically accurate and relevant as possible," Jackson told Bruce.

"I'll get back to you," Bruce said. "We're busy researching Doctor Miller's patients and Professor Miller's students. We'll find something for you. We're working as fast as we can."

"We know you are," Angela assured him. "Thanks."

They ended the call.

"Breakfast with the family?" Jackson said to Angela.

"Sounds lovely," she said.

They headed down. When they arrived, Stewart and Elizabeth were helping Nellie lay out the many dishes that made up her famous Irish breakfast.

Daniel was talking to Moira. The two were seated, and Moira was helping Daniel prepare his dish, warning him he didn't have much time before he had to head out for school.

"This is amazing. Again," Angela told Nellie when she appeared with a giant bowl of fluffy scrambled eggs cooked with bits of pepper, bacon crumbles, and cheese.

Nellie smiled. "Aye, lovie, thank you."

"I keep thinking," Moira said, smiling at Angela, "that when we do open as a hotel or bed and breakfast, we'll likely be world-famous with Nellie's amazing cooking."

Nellie smiled. "We be gettin' there, luv."

"Of course, we are," Moira agreed. She looked at Angela curiously but didn't say anything. Jackson had a feeling she'd want to talk to her cousin alone later.

"Can I do anything?" he asked.

"You may sit down and enjoy," Stewart told him. "Please." He grew serious as he took a seat himself. "We're grateful you're here. Well, we're not grateful there was a murder, but—"

He broke off.

"I was so upset I was driving everyone crazy," Moira said.

"The banshee," Elizabeth murmured.

"Okay, okay. I'm a little crazed," Moira admitted.

Jackson sat back and looked at Elizabeth. "I take it you don't believe n banshees?"

"Nor ghosties, spookies, leprechauns, or fairies," Elizabeth said. She shook her head. "And you're law enforcement. Scientists—"

"Oh, no, we are not scientists," Angela assured her. "But we have a wonderful forensic department with great scientists, and we've been incredibly impressed with the speed and accuracy of the department here. So, scientists have my total admiration."

"They would never believe in spookies, ghosties, or banshees," Elizabeth said knowingly. "I mean, I fully understand Mark Meadows and his ghost tours. They are very profitable, and if it helps the castle, I'm all for it."

Daniel reached across the table and put his hand on Moira's. "I'm so happy I get to live in a castle," he said.

Moira squeezed his hand. "And you are the best kid. I'm grateful you and your mom and dad live here."

Daniel grinned.

"Eat up," Elizabeth told her son. "We need to leave for school soon. Although, since there are no real steward duties today, maybe—"

"All right, all right. I'll drive Daniel to school," Stewart said, grinning. "No problem. Of course, if anyone needs anything, just let me know. I can make a stop on my way back."

"I think we're fine, thank you," Angela told him. "We can't eat any better than we are here."

"Right, excellent," Stewart said.

"How long have you been here?" Jackson asked him.

Stewart laughed. "Believe it or not, my dad worked for Colleen. When he retired, I took over."

"Stewart was already working here when we got married," Elizabeth said, smiling in remembrance.

"And when I was born," Daniel added.

"My grandfather worked here, too. Families have a way of going way, way back," Stewart told her.

"And I'm grateful," Moira said. "Stewart has a business degree with a minor in history. And that beats a theater and film degree when it comes to doing the right things to keep a castle afloat in the modern world."

"That's wonderful. Here's to both of you," Jackson said as he lifted his cup in a toast. "Or to all of you," he added, grinning at Elizabeth and Daniel.

"Thank you," Stewart said. "All right, lad, let's get going."

Daniel took one last bite and finished his eggs. He looked at Angela and Jackson and asked, "You'll still be here tonight, right?"

"Yes, we'll be here," Angela assured him.

He grinned and looked at his father, ready to head out.

"Back soon," Stewart said. He left the dining room with his hand o his son's shoulder as he propelled him forward.

On his way out, he looked at his watch as Moira looked at hers.

"Inspector McCray has arrived?" Angela asked. "Great watches. D they alert you both every time someone shows up?"

"No, only when they're let in. The gatehouse notifies us," Moira saic "If it's just a drop-off or the like, they don't bother notifying us."

Nellie walked back into the dining room. "The gatehouse. Time fo me to take a wee trip down there. I do have a bit of a problem cookin for small numbers."

Jackson laughed softly. "Small numbers? Nellie, you cooked breakfas for all of us—Moira, Angela, Stewart, Elizabeth, Daniel, me, and hope…you. Certainly a greater number than the usual family," he told he

"I still like big numbers," she said. "In me mum's day, many a famil had eleven children or more. But since I have so much, I'll run a nic plate on out to Sam."

"Sam?" Jackson interrupted. "That fellow has really been workin overtime."

"He's worried. He loves Moira like the rest of us do, and he' dedicated," Elizabeth told them.

"Very dedicated. But even the most devoted man needs sleep, and it' not that easy being the guard at a gatehouse when you're sleeping, Angela pointed out.

"Ah, well, you see," Nellie started, "no one gets through the gat without the gatehouse keeper pressing the right button. And if the guard fall asleep, they're hunched over the board. The gatehouse locks, and th glass was just put in a year ago and is bulletproof," she assured them.

Jackson looked at Moira. "Were you expecting something bad t happen? I mean, this isn't the Wild West like the U.S. You neede bulletproof glass?"

Moira waved a hand in the air. "Stewart did most of the work wit the company. It was just as cost-effective to use that glass. And wh knows?" She smiled, but it quickly faded. "No, all the bulletproof glass i the world wouldn't have helped Mrs. Robertson."

"Moira, we're on it," Jackson assured her as he rose to walk acros the hall to the Great Tower.

He'd thought Angela would be right behind him.

She wasn't. But then he remembered Moira's look, as if she wanted to speak with Angela. And Angela, of course, would want to know what her cousin wasn't saying.

He opened the large doors to the Great Tower and discovered that Inspector Angus McCray had indeed arrived.

"Welcome," Jackson told him. "If we hurry, I think Nellie might have left some breakfast out. That woman is a trooper. She always wants to make sure the guards have eaten, too," Jackson said.

"Nice. Aye, she's a fine old bird. She's been here for as long as I can remember," McCray said lightly. Then his tone changed. "Have you gotten anything?" he asked anxiously.

Jackson shrugged. "Well, we've gotten the fact that no one bought a pet poison dart frog with a credit card, but I still think the lab robbery down in the Amazon has something to do with this. I'm just trying to figure out what."

"Not just someone's pet? I mean, they could have missed something, right? We use cash in Ireland sometimes, and I've been to the States, so…"

"Yes, people do use cash. Our people have gone through the credit cards, and now they're sifting through all the security camera footage and traffic cams they can find."

"That's good. That's good. Still, it's hard to imagine someone buying a toxic frog and fooling with it enough to create the tiny patches. I mean, you wouldn't be wantin' to touch the damn things, would you? And to properly manage any of that, you'd truly need to know what you were doing, right?" McCray asked.

"I would assume," Jackson said with little more to give the inspector.

"And the household," Angus said, shaking his head. "I can't imagine. We did what you all call wellness checks on Colleen while Moira was getting everything together to move in with her granny. These people here…they're all so loyal. The thought that someone might be involved is hardly imaginable."

And yet still not just possible, but probable. Jackson thought.

He was saved from having to give the man an answer.

As if on cue, his phone rang.

Bruce. He excused himself and answered.

"You find something?" he asked.

"I did."

"Bruce. What?" Jackson demanded.

"All right. We discovered you were right. Adam paved the way again, getting me through to one of the cops who worked the robbery. They're um…well, they don't have the resources down there that we do. And they've never discovered who broke into the laboratory. The lab was a good thing—children sometimes get poisoned. Working on a real antidote was a great undertaking. But as we all know, labs sometimes use animals. And at that lab, they used rats for testing."

"I feel sorry for the rats," Jackson said. "But, Bruce—"

"I'm getting there as quickly as I can while explaining and making sense," Bruce assured him. "Rats are small. And that transdermal patch Angela found was small—teeny-tiny given the images you sent along and the description. The thing of it is, Jackson, they had to be small. The tiny patches were being used on the rats, each dosed with the poison dart frog toxin and in different doses."

"So, the patch did come from the Amazon lab," Jackson said.

"Yes. The authorities down there are worried sick. When the lab was inventoried after the robbery, they discovered that five of the tiny patches were missing. Tiny, Jackson. Because they were made for rodents, not Barbie and Ken dolls. Rats. And the doses were high because the antidote was being tested."

"So, someone who lived in South America or visited somewhere along the Amazon was in on that robbery," Jackson murmured.

"That's what you were thinking, right?"

"Yeah, it is. Now we need to discover who was there and who that person has seen since that might have shown up in Ireland."

"Something else, Jackson," Bruce said.

"What's that?"

"Whoever stole the patches could wind up being in trouble themselves."

"What do you mean?"

"As I said, five of the patches were stolen. But when the inventory was checked, the antidote doses were all still there. There are four more of those patches floating around somewhere, without the antidote. And I'm willing to bet the ones with the poison are in Ireland. Maybe even at the castle itself."

Chapter 8

"You've seen her, haven't you?" Moira asked Angela.

"Pardon?" Angela said, stalling. They sat together on the bed in the room Angela was sharing with Jackson, far from any others who might overhear.

Moira smiled. "I hear her," she said softly. "But you saw her. Oh, don't worry. I've done my research on you and your Krewe of Hunters."

"Officially, we're not the Krewe of Hunters. We are a specialized unit within the bureau."

"*The X-Files*," Moira said.

Angela grinned and shook her head. "*Most* things in the sky are unidentified, as far as I'm concerned. Though a friend at NASA told me we've created tons of space garbage that's swirling around above the atmosphere. Go figure. People creating garbage."

"Not *The X-Files*," Moira said. "But you go in when there are cult killings, when strange things happen around murders, and when bizarre rumors spread that may or may not be true. Angela, please, just tell me. Don't let me think I'm crazy. There is a banshee here, right?"

Angela hesitated for just a second before nodding. "She's sweet and beautiful, Moira. She lived here hundreds of years ago, and she's here to help people, not frighten them."

"Banshees lament," Moira said softly. "But that night, she was…it was more like screaming. Tell me, does she know what happened?"

Angela let out a long breath. "No. She senses things and felt that Amelia Robertson was in trouble. And…"

Her voice trailed off.

"What? Angela, please."

"Okay, first, you should know she loved Colleen and thinks the world of you."

"That's nice. But?"

"As I said, she said she senses things. When Mrs. Robertson was killed, she sensed evil."

"Evil?" Moira whispered. "But we're trying so hard to do all the right things here. To honor all the history that has passed in the long years these walls have stood on this land."

"She knows that."

"Then?"

"All right. Remember, we're in the middle of an investigation. But we do have suspects."

"They're gone? They're not in the castle?"

"They are not in the castle."

"But you can't do anything about them."

Angela let out a breath. "We're working on it," she assured her cousin.

"Mark is innocent of anything evil, you know," Moira said, staring hard into Angela's eyes.

"I didn't say he was guilty."

"But I know you are suspicious of him."

"Moira, honestly, Mark isn't coming off as suspicious to us."

"Then he's not one of your suspects?" Moira asked.

"Not particularly. Why?" Angela asked.

Moira was quiet for a minute. "Because I'm in love with him," she said at last.

Angela smiled softly. "It seemed to me there was something between you. I was thinking more that you two were attracted to each other, not that you were full-scale in love."

Moira laughed softly at that.

"It was a slow thing. He was doing some work here when Granny was still alive, and she was determined that we do what we needed to do. She truly was amazing. So much passion and energy—and love—packed into such a little body. She was about five feet tall and ninety pounds, but…wow. She could move mountains. She told me Irish women were born tough. That we were given that gift because of the years of bloodshed and warfare the country went through. But everything's good today. Ireland is great. You need to spend more time here."

Angela laughed. "Irish hospitality. And it does seem to be real."

"I've met incredible people in America, too."

Grinning, Angela told her, "Our Canadian cousins are known for being even nicer."

They both smiled, and Moira started to ask, "The banshee…?"

"She's beautiful. And she's determined to be a great guardian," Angela said, then hesitated. "I believe she'll warn us if anything else happens. We'll hear her if something is wrong. Her name was Lady Doreen Darien, and she lived hundreds of years ago. She died trying to stop an arrow from piercing her husband's heart to no avail. He died, too. In whatever afterlife there is, she sees him, but she loves her job as a banshee, trying to help the dead move on and the living deal with grief."

Moira smiled. "I wish I could see her."

"But you hear her. That's what's important," Angela said.

"Seriously, you heard Elizabeth this morning. I don't talk about her with any of them, even Nellie, who seems to believe in every legend out there. I mean, I guess I'm lucky to have the people who worked for Granny still here with me. Because taking all this over has been a lot. Stewart knows everything we need to hold on to the castle privately but also open it up for others. You couldn't ask for a better kid than Daniel. And while Elizabeth can be hard, she'd do just about anything for anyone.

"Lock-Stone has covered the gatehouse for a reasonable sum for a long time. You can't imagine what tourists sometimes want to do. Breaking into castles just for pictures or to chip away a block of old stone, and then… Well, you deal with it. North of here, they had a problem with a Tudor-era castle where people broke in to perform a rite. Though you guys deal with that stuff, so you probably know."

"Yeah. You don't want people just wandering around your property."

"Not to mention the liability. Even here." She sighed. "Thankfully, the thief died on the other side of the wall, but still. Oh, Angela. Why? It's so ridiculous for someone to think they could scale the wall and crawl over the metal spikes."

"Yes, it's bizarre. I agree. But you must always consider many things as the heiress to such a fine property," Angela said. "We're here for you."

Moira's watch buzzed. She glanced at Angela. "It's Mark."

"Does he know you're in love with him?" Angela asked.

"We've kept it pretty professional most of the time," Moira said. "But…"

"But?"

"I want him to stay here."

"You mean now, these next nights?"

Moira nodded. "I'm not sure if it has gone that far with him, but trust me, Angela. I did a fair amount of acting, as you know, most of it in th States. I met my share of men, some fawning, others with egos the size o the British Isles. But…"

"But?"

"The more I see Mark, the more I know," she said.

"Know what?" Angela asked.

"I think I want him to stay here forever."

"Oh." She drew out the word.

Angela desperately hoped Mark Meadows wasn't involved wit whatever was going on here.

And that her cousin wasn't in love with a calculating killer.

"Do you think having him stay now, while we're still trying to get t the bottom of what happened, is a good idea?" Angela asked.

"I'm telling you, Mark had nothing to do with any of this."

Angela nodded.

"You don't believe me. You know, I sense things, too," Moira said.

"I *do* believe you. It's just—"

"Right. You must be suspicious of everyone. I believe your husban and Inspector McCray are down in the Great Tower. They'll let Mark in."

"They will," Angela agreed. "But—"

"We should stay in the public spaces?" Moira asked dryly.

"It's just not a good time," Angela whispered.

"He's innocent."

"I hope so."

"Did the banshee sense he was evil?" Moira asked.

Angela sighed deeply and shook her head. "But there is sti something going on, Moira. Maybe if we catch the people who arrange for the patch and the murder, they'll tell us why this happened. Until ther please…"

"I know. Just be careful. Yes, I will. How did you know you coul trust Jackson when you first met him?" Moira asked.

"We were both asked to work on a case. We weren't the one threatened," Angela told her.

"Hmm. Trust for some people is hard. For others, it's natural."

"Moira—"

"Right. Okay. We'll play it your way. I'll head to the entertainmer room. I'll be there in full sight of anyone who peeks in."

Angela smiled. "I'm going to get on my computer and see what I ca dig up."

"You mean hack."

"I mean discover," Angela said.

Laughing, Moira rose, ready to leave the room. She stood by the door for a minute, listening.

Then she turned and smiled at Angela.

"Nothing will happen now," she said softly.

Angela smiled. "No," she agreed. "The banshee is silent."

Grinning, Moira left the room. Angela pulled out her laptop and wished she had all the resources she had back home. But Bruce had her mainframe with all its many apps she'd gained access to over the years—and the information none of them wanted traveling the world.

Still…

She was studying the Millers' social media when her phone rang. She smiled when she saw Jackson's name.

"I'm poring over social media, Jackson. Connie Miller keeps up conversations with her students. They talked a lot about South America. And…"

Her voice broke off.

"And?" he asked.

"Jackson, there's a conversation going on between her and a student named Antonio Ferrara. He's originally from Brazil, and they're discussing him going back to visit some of his family—along the Amazon," she told him.

"Is he back in the States?" Jackson asked her.

"He is."

"Bruce will get someone to wherever he is. She teaches in Georgia, right?"

"Yep. I don't have an address, though."

"Bruce will get it. I'm not sure if we have any agents in the area right now, but I want one of our people to question him. You're in the bedroom?"

"I am."

He hesitated. "I'll get back to you."

She ended the call and kept searching. There was nothing more, just a pleasant exchange between a teacher and a student who had returned from a trip. He talked about the beauty of Brazil and the power of the Amazon River.

Nothing more.

She went on another social media site.

There, she discovered a picture—one taken in front of a large mall.

A woman was in the photo, along with a man, and between them stood a boy of about seventeen.

There was a caption.

With brilliant student Antonio Ferrara.

Angela grappled for her phone again, eager to reach Jackson, but looked up to see him entering the room with Inspector McCray.

"Angela?"

"You're here. Look."

She turned the computer around so both men could see what she had found.

"And this kid—"

"Just came back from a trip to the Amazon in that picture. I've checked the dates. The timing of the break-in at the lab coincides with his visit to Brazil."

"It's a big country," Angus said.

"But I think it's enough to warrant a visit to Dr. and Professor Miller, don't you?" Angela asked.

"I do," Jackson said.

"We still need more than the fact that poison dart frogs come from the Amazon, and Professor Miller had a student there. That's entirely circumstantial," McCray said. "But I am happy to talk to the couple again. Maybe they'll realize we are coming closer to the truth and throw their accomplices under the proverbial bus if someone else is involved."

"We have agents in the area where the kid lives. Bruce will get them there."

"Perfect. I just need to tell Moira we're heading out," Angela said but then hesitated.

"You don't want to leave her here alone, do you?" Jackson asked her.

"No," Angela admitted.

"We can handle this," Jackson said, gesturing to McCray. "You never know. By the time we get to Dublin and reach the couple in their hotel room, I may have heard something from Bruce."

"I think I'm going to hang here with Moira and Mark," Angela said. "Just…"

"Yeah. We let him in when he arrived. No one else seemed to be around. I don't know if Stewart ever came back from dropping Daniel at school. We didn't see Nellie return from the gatehouse, either. Maybe she's enjoying herself in the fresh air. I assume Elizabeth is doing whatever she does when she gets a free morning," Jackson said. "We'll see you down to join Moira and Mark then take off."

"Okay," Angela agreed.

They found Moira and Mark sitting on the couch, heads close together, deep in discussion. But both looked up expectantly when the three of them entered the room. They both smiled when Jackson explained he and Angus were off to follow up on a lead, but that Angela was staying with them.

"Let's do this," Angus said to Jackson.

"Let's," he agreed.

The two men left the room, and Angela looked at Moira. She wondered if her cousin resented her for being there, watching over her when she was with the man she said she loved.

But Moira seemed happy enough to visit with them both.

"Mark, history was your major, right? That's really cool. I have to admit, the best stories in the world come from history," Angela said.

Mark smiled. "I love it, and not just Irish history. I can tell you things about America that will make your hair stand on end."

"I know a few of those stories, too," Angela said, chuckling.

"And sad stuff. Like here, sometimes. Wherever it occurs, a Civil War is the worst kind. Neighbors against neighbors, even sons and daughters against their parents, brothers against brothers. Like what happened in the America Civil War. But history is also full of cool stuff. Want to hear about happy stuff that comes up during the ghost tours?" he asked her.

Angela smiled and made herself comfortable in the plush chair across from the sofa.

"I'd love to," she said. "As long as I'm not interrupting. I didn't mean to intrude."

"It's great you're here," Mark assured her. "Of course, if I know Moira, she may fall asleep while I'm talking."

She gave him a light tap on the arm and a serious frown.

"Ouch! Just teasing," he assured her. "Okay, then. Cool history about people being good to one another. Hmm…"

* * * *

"Good to see Sam finally took a break," Angus said as he and Jackson drove out of the gate and headed toward the road to Dublin.

"It's curious that he can pick and choose his hours like he does," Jackson said.

"Oh, it's a small company. The same three men are always here. Weird schedules, though. They work long hours and have odd days off, kind of like some of the medical personnel I know. I dated a nurse once who worked four ten-hour days and then had three days off in a row. Now that would be nice," Angus said. He looked at Jackson. "The fact that I couldn't just take off for three-day holidays whenever I chose to didn't do a lot for our relationship, though."

"I'm not sure any of us in this business are ever really off," Jackson told him.

"That is very true. But you're here."

"We have great folks at our office," Jackson said simply. "And we have a European division now that comes in when asked, especially when there's an American connection in one way or another."

"So, Angela and Moira," McCray said. "Cousins?"

"Second cousins, but yes. Anyway, I suppose some would consider it a vacation to visit an Irish castle."

McCray laughed grimly. "Especially when someone there gets murdered by poison dart frog toxin."

Jackson shrugged. He liked McCray. It was easy to work with the man.

They continued to chat idly and were close to Dublin when Jackson received the call he'd been waiting for from back home.

"The kid spilled like a water faucet," Bruce said.

"What did he say?" Jackson asked. "Did he admit to breaking into the lab?"

"No, nothing like that. He said he met up with some, as he called them, *tough guys* who broke into the lab in Brazil. They had these sealed bags they didn't really know what to do with. Claimed they'd been looking for money or something to pawn, but all they found was a bunch of lousy frogs, vials, and those kinds of things. Anyway, this kid, Antonio Ferrara, was there with his parents and talked to our very own Axel Tiger, who was down in Georgia on a different assignment.

"The kid said he took the bag because he knew he had a cool teacher and thought maybe he could bring it to her and she would do something. They wanted a finders' fee, of course. But, anyway, Antonio gave the bag with the rat patches to that teacher—none other than Professor Connie Miller."

"All right, thanks. We're on our way to them now," Jackson told Bruce. He looked at McCray, repeating what he'd learned.

The inspector didn't look his way since he was driving, but he did smile.

"It's going to be a complicated case, but I think we've got enough to bring them in and hold them while we try to get something out of them or find some evidence," McCray said.

"Let's do it," Jackson agreed.

McCray was still smiling.

"What?"

"Well, I mean, we all know that not liking animals or children doesn't make a person evil, but... I don't know. I find it a good indicator."

"While not liking animals or children doesn't make a man or woman a murderer," Jackson said, "walking around with transdermal patches with poison dart frog toxin may."

"Why, though?"

"Maybe they'll tell us," Jackson said.

"Great," McCray said, pulling into the hotel's small parking lot. "My men are here, right in front, watching over them. I can guarantee the couple hasn't fled."

"Good thing," Jackson said.

He nodded when Angus introduced him to the two men on duty, and hen they headed in. Doctor and Professor Miller were on the second floor in room 212.

But when they knocked, they got no reply.

Angus looked at Jackson.

"This is Inspector McCray," he called. "We need to speak with you again."

Again, no answer.

"Think they're taking a romantic shower?" Angus asked Jackson.

"Your country...but I suggest we break down the door. I mean...was hat a scream I heard? Exigent circumstances, right?" He looked at Angus with a raised brow.

McCray nodded. "On three...one, two, three!"

They both gave the door a hard kick.

As they entered, Jackson knew the couple wouldn't be telling them anything.

Chapter 9

Mark knew a great deal about not just Irish history but world history. H
regaled Angela with tales about the United States, giving her little-know
facts about the Revolution, the War of 1812, the Civil War, and mor
Which was impressive, because she knew a lot of history, herself.

Listening to him made for a nice afternoon. Nellie checked on the
all and offered them little potpies for lunch. They spent some time wit
her at the dining room table, as well as Elizabeth and Stewart when the
emerged.

It all seemed congenial and pleasant.

They didn't bring up the murder, other than when Angela informe
them all that Jackson and Angus were off following a lead that might b
nothing.

After lunch, she excused herself and stepped out into the courtyar
wondering if the banshee might appear during the daytime.

But she wasn't there.

When Angela returned to the entertainment room, she discovere
that Moira and Mark were no longer there. Trying not to feel panicky, sh
called Moira's phone, half-expecting her cousin not to answer.

But she did.

"I'm fine. Promise. I'm with Mark. We're in my room."

"Moira…"

"Here. Talk to him," Moira said. The next thing Angela heard wa
Mark's voice.

"I swear to you, Angela, on everything that's holy, I would rather di
than harm Moira. I'm innocent, and you know we're together. If anythin
were to happen to her now, you'd arrest me on the spot. We're good,

promise," Mark said.

"Not to mention we're over twenty-one and able to do as we please, so lay off," Moira called. "Wait. I didn't mean that. Please, don't get mad at me. I want you here. We *need* you here. I'm just stressed."

"It's okay," Angela said. "Just know I'll be right next door. I'm going to get back on my computer there," she told them.

She wasn't sure what she wanted to do, and she only stared at the blank screen for several minutes. All right, they'd followed some good leads. Of course, the couple might plead their innocence, and they might be looking at only circumstantial evidence right now, but given what they did have, it looked like the Millers were guilty.

"Why?" she murmured out loud. She winced, knowing her cousin was in the next room with a man who had accumulated wealth and could afford the castle if she were to sell. But…

Moira had admitted to her—and possibly him—that she was in love with him. So, logically, he could marry her and get it that way. And if he wasn't in love, he could take his time and rid himself of her.

But Angela didn't believe that. She wasn't perfect, but she was usually good at reading people.

So…

She wrote a page to herself about all those involved with the castle.

Stewart and Elizabeth McKenna and their son, Daniel.

Nellie Antrim.

Lock-Stone Security. The people who manned the gatehouse. But unlike Stewart and Nellie, they hadn't been here forever. And they were just paid for a nice, cushy gig.

Still…

She put down Lock-Stone. After she did, she looked up the company. It was small. There were only four employees, Sam Hall, the man they knew; Oscar Murphy, Elijah Blake, and Brian Carson, the manager. The company had taken a few other jobs and received five-star write-ups from old customers.

She wondered who owned the company and started to dig to find out. She had just begun her search when she received Jackson's call.

"What happened? Did they admit anything? Did they talk?" she asked.

"No. They couldn't talk. The good doctor and professor are dead. Their bodies are on the way to the morgue."

"No." She put a hand to her mouth. "You don't think they were killed by—?"

"Two of the missing transdermal patches were here," Jackson said "This time, the killer didn't even remove them."

"And it wasn't done by choice?"

"You really think those two would have taken their lives? I sure as hell don't," Jackson said. "Angela, be careful. We're on our way back There are still two of those little patches out there. It's likely the Millers managed to get that patch onto Mrs. Robertson, but whoever is pulling the strings probably knew the Millers would get caught and feared they might spill everything. You need to be extremely careful. Someone at that castle murdered the Millers."

* * * *

They weren't far out, but by the time all the proper authorities had arrived, putting two branches of the Irish police with forensics and the medical examiner, Jackson was more than antsy.

He was nearly in a panic to get back to Angela.

He reminded himself again that she was a competent and capable agent. She could kick ass.

But neither her prowess with a gun nor her many talents in martial arts would be of any use if someone just sidled by and…

And set one of the lethal patches on her skin.

Won't happen. Wouldn't happen so fast. If anyone at the castle is guilty, they won't dare kill again today. It would be too obvious. And with so few people…

Finally, he and Angus were back in the car. It seemed obvious the inspector was an empathetic man since he glanced at Jackson and maneuvered the vehicle with speed and skill, not trying to talk much until they were halfway there.

"Who?" he demanded. "Who? And why? I don't begin to understand."

"Someone really wants that castle," Jackson surmised.

"Then why not just kill Moira?" Angus asked.

"Too obvious?" Jackson suggested. He shook his head. "To make her miserable enough that she'd be ready to…?"

"Sell out cheaply?"

Jackson shrugged. "Well, we have people digging into financials But…"

"I'm lost. How did someone at the castle enlist the Miller couple to find a kid going to Brazil, manage to get the lab broken into, and then kill a random tourist?"

"Long-term planning, I imagine," Jackson said. "When did Colleen die?" he asked.

"About a year and a half ago," Angus told him.

"Maybe this has been in the works since," Jackson said. He leaned against the seat. "Five transdermal patches. The murderer hoped to get away with the first death being ruled natural. Then…"

"Something else was supposed to happen to someone else. When it did, Moira would be so distraught she would just want out," Angus finished. He was smiling grimly. "Whoever it is doesn't know Moira. She won't give up on her Granny's dream that easily."

"No, she's not the kind to give up," Jackson agreed. He looked over at McCray. "We need to figure this out now."

"Of course, we do," Angus agreed.

"No. I mean right now. As in tonight."

"And how…?"

"I have a plan," Jackson assured him.

When they neared the castle, he put a call through to Angela.

She could get the ball rolling.

* * * *

Ending her call with Jackson, Angela hesitated for just a minute. She thought about knocking on her cousin's door but opted to call instead.

Moira answered right away.

"We'll celebrate tonight," Angela said.

"What? They found out what happened to Mrs. Robertson?"

"They were on their way to arrest Doctor and Professor Miller when they found the two of them dead. They must have known the police were closing in. They killed themselves," Angela said.

Angela felt horrible lying to Moira.

But she needed to lie to them all if they were to execute Jackson's plan.

She heard Moira's joyous cry as she told Mark about the call and that the killers had been caught.

"I'm going to get downstairs and tell Nellie, Stewart, and Elizabeth. And…well, I'm sure Nellie has dinner planned already, but it will be a real celebration. I'll bet she has some champagne on the premises. It's time to drink it," Angela said cheerfully.

"We'll be down soon," Moira promised.

Angela hurried downstairs, racing into the kitchen to find Nellie.

"Hey," she said happily.

"Hello," Nellie replied. "Ye look so happy, lass."

"I am. The killers were caught. God knows why, but the Millers killed Mrs. Robertson. Anyway, tonight, you will join us at the table. We'll all help you get everything out, and we'll all clean up, but after some delicious champagne. I'm hoping we have some."

"Aye, we do. We do." Nellie nodded. "Oh, wonder of wonders. Thankfully, you and your hubby were here, lassie."

Angela smiled. "Off to tell Stewart and Elizabeth."

"Our meal will be ready in an hour," Nellie said.

"Perfect. We'll be here to help in thirty minutes," Angela promised.

She raced back up the stairs, tapping on the McKenna's door.

Stewart opened it, and Angela saw he'd been doing homework with his son.

"Celebration," she said.

"What?" Stewart asked.

"It's celebration time. The inspector and Jackson found the Millers dead—by their own patches. We don't know why yet, but they killed Mrs. Robertson. They likely knew they were going to be caught and offed themselves." Angela hated using death by suicide as an excuse, especially added to a lie. "Oh, that doesn't sound good for a celebration, does it? But...well, the killers are gone, and business can go back to normal. That's something to celebrate."

"It's all wonderful," Stewart said but winced. "Well, the whole thing is *horrible*, but at least it's solved."

"Nellie said to be down in an hour," Angela told him.

"I'll get down there and help serve—"

"Not to worry tonight. Jackson and I will take care of it," she promised. Angela saw Daniel watching her and felt her stomach tighten. "I didn't even think. Daniel may be a bit young for the champagne."

"We'll give our lad a wee sip," Stewart said happily.

Angela smiled and hurried down the hall, anxious to get back downstairs. When she arrived in the kitchen, she discovered Angus and Jackson were already there.

"We're kitchen help," Angus said.

"And good at it, mind you," Jackson told her.

Their gazes met, and Nellie beamed. "Grab the covered dishes there, me fine lads. We'll get this party moving."

Angela glanced at the inspector, fully aware he knew about Jackson's plan to bring them all together and put a few ideas to the test.

McCray could have been an actor, she thought. But then someone else in his house would have been great on stage, too.

Because more had been discovered during the forensic accounting, and Jackson had a real suspect in mind.

Angela hadn't had much of a chance to dig, but apparently, Bruce had looked in the right place.

The chatter as they all worked to set the dining table in splendor was fun and lively. Of course, they knew not to get close to anyone.

Because two of those little patches were still out there.

Soon enough, the table was set.

"Did you call Sam?" Angela asked Nellie. "He's been so wonderful. He should be here for this."

"I called him, but he said he had plans. Told me he was extremely happy all was well, lass," Nellie told her.

"Great."

"All right. Let's do this," Moira cried, pouring champagne for the group. The McKenna family had opted for bubbling ginger ale for Daniel, but he, too, had a glass ready to raise.

"To all of you. My dear friends, family by all we have created, thank you for being by my side through so much that has been so horrible. Dear, dear friends, all seeking to make Granny's dream come true. Nellie, Stewart, Elizabeth, Daniel. Thank you. And Mark, you've helped so much with your tours. And, of course, Inspector McCray. And last but never least, my American cousin, Angela Hawkins Crow, and Jackson. Thank you for finding the truth."

"Here, here!" Jackson cried.

"Sláinte," Angela toasted.

"Great. She's turning Irish," Stewart said.

They sat. They ate.

Chatted…

And then Jackson spoke. "Just one thing. I'm still so curious. Why would the Millers want to kill Mrs. Robertson? Stewart, did you know hem? I understand you were in Georgia about nine months ago for a quickie vacation."

"What?" Stewart said. "No, I—I have an American cousin in Savannah. I never met the Millers. I never met them at all, even here."

He seemed truly lost.

"Just curious," Jackson said lightly and laughed. "Our states aren't hat big, and I'm guessing you might think the castle should be yours."

"Wait. What?" Stewart seemed truly perplexed. And angry.

"Ah, me good lad, quit with the nasties," Nellie said. "I'll be grabbir another bottle of champagne."

She rose and started to walk by Stewart and Daniel—perhaps a littl too close. There *were* still patches missing.

Nellie?

They could take no chances. Not with a kid's life.

And just as the thought struck her, Angela heard it.

The cry of the banshee.

"No!" she screamed, standing up and causing everyone to freeze.

Even Jackson stared at her.

But Moira didn't. She'd heard it, too.

Nellie? The sweet and kind housekeeper? Fiftyish, small…

"Back off. Get away from him, Nellie," Angela cried.

But even as the housekeeper stared at her, there was a whoosh c movement, and Sam Hall was suddenly there, pulling Daniel out of hi chair and causing the boy to scream in terror.

"What a pain in the arse you people have proven to be," Sam saic smiling wickedly as he showed them one of the patches he held just a ha inch from the boy's neck. "We'll be leaving, Nellie, the boy, and me. An when we're safe, I'll let him go—"

"You and Nellie?" Moira said incredulously.

"What the bloody hell difference does it make now, ye've gone an destroyed it all!" Nellie shouted at him. "You didn't ha' ta give 'em m name."

"Nellie?" Moira repeated.

"The castle is mine. Mine, do you hear me? I've worked and cared fc her forever. She's mine. And don't you go getting any ideas," Nellie saic "I've a will, signed by yer granny herself, Miss Moira. I needed the righ time—"

"No. No way," Moira said. "My grandmother wanted Castle Darie to stay in the family. She believed I'd have children and it would stay i the family for generations. She loved you. She gave you all the time o you wanted. She got anything you needed. How could you? Oh, my Goc You knew her handwriting. You forged a will."

By then, Jackson was up, but Sam turned to shout at him. "Stay bacl unless you want a dead kid on your hands."

"Let it go. Let the castle go. Let anything go but my son," Elizabet cried.

"We have no intention of losing Daniel," Jackson said. "Just do wha you want. But leave the boy out of it. If you want to threaten someon threaten me."

"I'll not be messing with a U.S. agent, but put your guns on the table. Now," Sam ordered.

"Ye've ruined everything!" Nellie shouted again.

"Take me, then," Angela said, moving closer to Sam.

"No. Take me," Moira pleaded. "I'm the cause of all of this, or so it seems. Nellie has a will, and she forged Granny's signature. She was good at it. She signed so many things for my grandmother through the years. Take me, Sam. I'm an actress. No hidden skills, no strength to punch you or take you by surprise and…and if you don't get what you want…well, kill me, and the castle is up for grabs."

"You have two patches," Jackson said. "You can't kill us all. Let the boy go. Take one of us."

"No, the kid will be no trouble."

"You let him go, and I'll put my gun on the table," Jackson said.

"Stupid Americans, always armed," Sam muttered.

"This whole thing was a plan between you to get the castle. That's why Nellie was always so nice to bring you food and tell you how things were going. And why you took on so many shifts at the castle. A strange, convoluted plan," Angela said. "First, you drowned an elderly man. Then you saw a thief and figured it was a great opportunity. Then, to *really* throw Moira off, you killed a tourist. Make her inheritance seem cursed, right? Wow. But seriously, what a dumb plan."

"Nothing dumb about it," Sam snapped. "Nellie could keep me updated on what was happening here, and I managed the rest. She deserves this place. We'll be married. I'd have the money to give poor Moira something. We'd have made the lord and lady of the castle functioning caretakers. It would have been ours," Sam snapped.

"Sam, ye're an idiot," Nellie snapped. "We'd have made it if you hadn't barged in—"

"Remember, Nellie. I have two patches," Sam reminded her angrily. "In fact, at this point, old girl, you're nothing but baggage. The boy and I are leaving."

"What?" Nellie demanded. "Aye, we're in a mess, we are. So, ye'd throw me to the wolves? You care nothing for me. You only want to be lord of the castle."

"Shut up," Sam roared but then sneered at Nellie. "I'd have taken care of you, too. In the end."

"Bastard. A title would ne'er make ye a lord," Nellie raged.

"Leave Daniel. Take me," Moira cried.

By then, the banshee's screeching was almost painful to Angela's ears

"She's coming for someone," Angela announced.

"Who?" Sam demanded.

"The banshee. You can't hear her?" Angela asked.

Sam told them all what they could do with themselves and started backing out of the room, dragging the sobbing boy along with him.

"Don't move," he warned. "If you do, the kid will die."

And then he was out, heading down the hallway with the screaming child.

Stewart started after him instantly, but Jackson caught him. "Wait We must, we have to take him unawares. Please. Let Angela and I do this For your son's life."

Stewart held back, sobbing. Jackson glanced at Angela, and they silently headed after the man who was dragging the child along.

Luckily, he didn't close the Great Tower door completely. And when he moved, he headed toward the gate, which as their security guard, he could easily open.

But it was dark, and despite the outdoor lights and the waning moon they could follow silently behind him on each side.

He stopped once and looked back.

Then, Angela decided to mimic the banshee, keeping well-hidden behind a bush and letting out her cry of distress.

The man heard her strange howling and froze for a minute. And then Angela saw her. The banshee.

The real banshee was there, ready to help them.

She moved toward Sam, floating above the ground in her cloud of darkness. Suddenly, she shouted, "See me, see me, see me, Samuel Hall!"

He might not have seen her, but he felt her, and it caused him to pause and look back, shivering, sensing the unseen danger. And as the banshee stepped toward him, almost as if she would seep right into him he shuddered violently and eased his hold on the boy so the deadly patch was far from his flesh.

It was enough.

Angela tore from her bush, slamming into young Daniel and rolling with him far from Sam as Jackson stepped forward, his gun aimed at the man.

"Don't move. Wild American, you know? Trigger-happy. Though maybe not. I hate like hell to kill people, but after this murder spree of yours, I might not have that much trouble."

By then, McCray was out, hurrying to stand by Jackson.

"How the hell do we get the patches from him?" McCray asked. He shivered as if he, too, sensed something in the yard. Something…

Not evil. Just…there.

"Well, I can shoot him. Or—"

Jackson didn't have to shoot him. The man suddenly let out a shout of terror and slapped his hands against his face.

Both patches landed against his cheeks, and he went down to his knees, shrieking and screaming.

"I'm calling an ambulance; it's the right thing to do," McCray said.

"Indeed, it is," Jackson agreed.

The banshee moved near Angela and the still-sobbing child. "The right thing. But it will do no good. As evil as he is, I will bring him where he will learn about the error of his ways."

"Thank you," Angela whispered to her.

The banshee turned and smiled at her. "Thank you for seeing me."

"You saved his life."

"No, I gave *you* the chance to save his life," the banshee said. With a smile, she was gone, drifting across the space between them and Sam before plucking something ethereal from the man's body.

Soon after, Angela realized that Moira was standing near her as she tried to calm the sobbing boy.

She stared after the banshee, smiling.

"I can see her," she whispered. "She is so beautiful. The ghost from my dreams. And I know she will be with me here for years and years. Thank you."

The banshee lowered her head, smiling and accepting the praise.

Stewart and Elizabeth came out, in tears as they rushed to Daniel.

Then, sirens cut through the night.

Epilogue

"I still can't believe they caused so much pain and misery with such a confused and convoluted plan," Angela said.

Jackson rolled over. "Nellie wanted the castle in the worst way. She felt it was owed to her. And Sam Hall wanted to be more than he was. He wanted a title more than anything in the world, something that got stuck in his head. We can look into it more, I suppose. Bad childhood? We've learned that many things, such as low self-esteem, can cause such twists in the human mind. And while I don't know what was behind Sam's desperation to be the lord of such a place, he and Nellie, odd as it may sound, apparently started something while Moira's granny was still alive. They were a couple, but he would have sacrificed her, too. They needed a plan. If Nellie had immediately produced the will, Moira would have fought it. Their goal was to make Moira so miserable she'd be ready to give it all up."

"So they killed all those people."

"Apparent suicide, an accident. And they wanted a tourist to die, seemingly of natural causes. But they had four more patches," Jackson said.

"How—?"

"Sam. We never checked on Sam's comings and goings. He found out that despite their illustrious careers, the Millers were drowning in debt. He discovered all that by being almost as good on the web as you are. Doctor Miller was facing a malpractice suit, and Sam threatened to say he'd also seen the man, was treated off the books, and nearly died."

Jackson scratched at his scruff. "So, the Millers were roped into the plot. All they had to do was get the frog toxin. When they arrived with it, they learned Sam would kill them if they didn't get close to a guest. So, they did. But we suspected them, and Sam caught on. That's why he suddenly wasn't working. The man was a security expert. He could easily get by the police at the hotel. And with them gone, he planned to go along with the celebration and then wait a bit and kill someone else. When Moira was truly miserable, Nellie would produce the will and offer to take the place off her hands. Subtly threatening, of course, that she would do so one way or the other. But they didn't plan for Moira's American cousin—and her husband, of course," Jackson added, grinning.

"So horrible," Angela said but leaned back.

It was over.

Moira was still devastated that people she loved and trusted had come up with such a horrible and twisted scheme, but she had Mark with her.

And they were doing very well.

The paperwork had taken days and happened in Ireland and the United States, but they'd had time between the tie-up work to visit St. Patrick's Cathedral, Dublin Castle, Temple Bar, and more.

Angela would always love Ireland. And, yes, it was great to have a cousin who owned a castle.

But now they were lying on a gorgeous beach in Hawaii, arranged with some help from the McFadden brothers, Mary, and of course, Adam.

Angela felt the sun's warmth and took a moment to realize she cherished her life. She was lucky.

No, she didn't have a castle.

But she had a man who loved her, a job that made her feel as if she mattered, her children, and she was rich in ways so many others might never know.

"We do have to go back, you know," she said, rolling to looked into Jackson's eyes.

"We will."

"I'm not sure I thanked the banshee enough," she said.

He smiled. "Just the banshee?" he queried.

She laughed, smacked him on the shoulder, and raced for the surf.

He ran after her.

And she knew.

He always would.

* * * *

Also from 1001 Dark Nights and Heather Graham, discover Crimson Twilight, When Irish Eyes Are Haunting, All Hallows Eve, Blood on the Bayou, Hallow Be The Haunt, Haunted Be the Holidays, Blood Night, The Dead Heat of Summer, Haunted House, and Descend to Darkness.

Sign up for the 1001 Dark Nights Newsletter
and be entered to win a Tiffany Key necklace.

There's a contest every month!

Go to www.1001DarkNights.com to subscribe.

As a bonus, all subscribers can download
FIVE FREE exclusive books!

Discover 1001 Dark Nights Collection Ten

DRAGON LOVER by Donna Grant
A Dragon Kings Novella

KEEPING YOU by Aurora Rose Reynolds
An Until Him/Her Novella

HAPPILY EVER NEVER by Carrie Ann Ryan
A Montgomery Ink Legacy Novella

DESTINED FOR ME by Corinne Michaels
A Come Back for Me/Say You'll Stay Crossover

MADAM ALANA by Audrey Carlan
A Marriage Auction Novella

DIRTY FILTHY BILLIONAIRE by Laurelin Paige
A Dirty Universe Novella

HIDE AND SEEK by Laura Kaye
A Blasphemy Novella

TANGLED WITH YOU by J. Kenner
A Stark Security Novella

TEMPTED by Lexi Blake
A Masters and Mercenaries Novella

THE DANDELION DIARY by Devney Perry
A Maysen Jar Novella

CHERRY LANE by Kristen Proby
A Huckleberry Bay Novella

THE GRAVE ROBBER by Darynda Jones
A Charley Davidson Novella

CRY OF THE BANSHEE by Heather Graham
A Krewe of Hunters Novella

DARKEST NEED by Rachel Van Dyken
A Dark Ones Novella

CHRISTMAS IN CAPE MAY by Jennifer Probst
A Sunshine Sisters Novella

A VAMPIRE'S MATE by Rebecca Zanetti
A Dark Protectors/Rebels Novella

WHERE IT BEGINS by Helena Hunting
A Pucked Novella

Also from Blue Box Press

THE MARRIAGE AUCTION by Audrey Carlan

THE JEWELER OF STOLEN DREAMS by M.J. Rose

SAPPHIRE STORM by Christopher Rice writing as C. Travis Rice
A Sapphire Cove Novel

ATLAS: THE STORY OF PA SALT by Lucinda Riley and Harry Whittaker

A SOUL OF ASH AND BLOOD by Jennifer L. Armentrout
A Blood and Ash Novel

START US UP by Lexi Blake
A Park Avenue Promise Novel

LOVE ON THE BYLINE by Xio Axelrod
A Plays and Players Novel

FIGHTING THE PULL by Kristen Ashley
A River Rain Novel

A FIRE IN THE FLESH by Jennifer L. Armentrout
A Flesh and Fire Novel

Discover More Heather Graham

Descend to Darkness: A Krewe of Hunters Novella

Angela Hawkins Crow awakens to find herself in total darkness. Despite her years as a Krewe agent, she is first seized with panic, but her life and her training kick in. She knows that she must stay calm and go back in her mind to find out how she got where she is…and where she might be.

Meanwhile, an eerie phone call comes in at Krewe headquarters, warning them all that Angela has been kidnapped, describing her ordeal, and lamenting the fact that she can't be saved.

But there is no such thing with the Krewe. In the dark and in the light, the fight is on.

Angela determines that she might know what has happened to her, and she is prepared when her kidnapper can't resist the temptation to check in on her.

By following his wife's expertise with research, Jackson discovers what just might be happening—and in the darkness of night and the silence of the graveyard, he'll risk everything to find the woman he loves.

* * * *

Haunted House: A Krewe of Hunters Novella

Halloween! Strange things are going to happen and every year, while loving the holiday, members of the Krewe of Hunters also dread it.

Something somewhere is bound to happen.

And it does.

Krewe member Jon Dickson's fiancée Kylie Connelly is contacted by an old friend who has just moved to Salem, Massachusetts, when the unimaginable happens as the holiday approaches.

Jenny Auger has just managed to buy the historic home of her dreams. But it comes with far more history than she ever imagined—the skeletal remains of seven victims interred in the old walls of the house years and years before—along with a threatening curse.

And strange things are happening in the city. Bizarre attacks… murders that mimic days of old.

With Halloween on the way.

Kylie has a history with the city of Salem, and her strange talent for being within the minds of those under attack—first realized in the city—remains sharp.

But the situation is far more dire than what they have discovered, with strange events and attacks occurring.

And with all their talent for crime solving—with help from the living and the dead—it still remains to be seen if they can solve the murders of he past before Halloween, and the bloodbath that just might occur if the ins of a time gone by cannot be brought to light.

* * * *

The Dead Heat of Summer: A Krewe of Hunters Novella

Casey Nicholson has always been a little bit sensitive, and she puts it to use in her shop in Jackson Square, where she reads tarot cards and tea leaves. She's not a medium, but she *can* read people well.

When the ghost of Lena Marceau comes to her in the cemetery, shedding tears and begging for help, Casey's at first terrified and then determined. Lena knows she was the victim of a malicious murder. Assumes her husband was, as well, and now fears that her daughter and sister are also in danger. And all over what she believes is someone's quest o control Marceau Industries, the company left to Lena's late husband.

Casey isn't sure how she can help Lena. She isn't an investigator or with any arm of law enforcement. But when she receives a visit from a all, dark and very handsome stranger—ironically an FBI agent—she realizes that she's being drawn into a deadly game where she must discover the truth or possibly die trying.

Special Agent Ryder McKinley of the Krewe of Hunters has his own strange connection to the case. Hoping to solve the mystery of his cousin's death, he arrives at Casey's shop during his hunt for answers and finds something wholly unexpected. He fears that Casey's involvement puts her in danger, yet she's already knee-deep in deadly waters. Unfortunately, there's nothing to do but follow the leads and hope they don't also fall prey to the vicious and very human evil hunting his family.

* * * *

Blood Night: A Krewe of Hunters Novella

Any member of the Krewe of Hunters is accustomed to the strang
And to conversing now and then with the dead.

For Andre Rousseau and Cheyenne Donegal, an encounter with th
deceased in a cemetery is certainly nothing new.

But this year, Halloween is taking them across the pond–
unofficially.

Their experiences in life haven't prepared them for what's to come.

Cheyenne's distant cousin and dear friend Emily Donegal has calle
from London. Murder has come to her neighborhood, with bodies jus
outside Highgate Cemetery, drained of blood.

The last victim was found at Emily's doorstep, and evidence seems t
be arising not just against her fiancé, Eric, but against Emily, too. Bu
Emily isn't just afraid of the law—many in the great city are beginning t
believe that the historic Vampire of Highgate is making himself know
aided and abetted by adherents. Some are even angry and frightene
enough to believe they should take matters into their own hands.

Andre and Cheyenne know they're in for serious trouble when the
arrive, and they soon come to realize that the trouble might be deadly nc
just for Emily and Eric, but for themselves as well.

There's help to be found in the beautiful and historic old cemetery.

And as All Hallows Eve looms, they'll be in a race against tim
seeking the truth before the infamous vampire has a chance to strik
again.

* * * *

Haunted Be the Holidays: A Krewe of Hunters Novella

When you're looking for the victim of a mysterious murder in
theater, there is nothing like calling on a dead diva for help! Krew
members must find the victim if they're to discover the identity of
murderer at large, one more than willing to kill the performers when h
doesn't like the show.

It's Halloween at the Global Tower Theatre, a fantastic and histor
theater owned by Adam Harrison and run by spouses of Krewe member
During a special performance, a strange actor makes an appearance in th
middle of the show, warning of dire events if his murder is not solve
before another holiday rolls around.

Dakota McCoy and Brodie McFadden dive into the mystery. Both have a. special talent for dealing with ghosts, but this one is proving elusive. With the help of Brodie's diva mother and his ever-patient father—who were killed together when a stage chandelier fell upon them—Dakota and Brodie set out to solve the case.

If they can't solve the murder quickly, there will be no Thanksgiving for the Krewe...

* * * *

Hallow Be the Haunt: A Krewe of Hunters Novella

Years ago, Jake Mallory fell in love all over again with Ashley Donegal—while he and the Krewe were investigating a murder that replicated a horrible Civil War death at her family's Donegal Plantation.

Now, Ashley and Jake are back—planning for their wedding, which will take place the following month at Donegal Plantation, her beautiful old antebellum home.

But Halloween is approaching and Ashley is haunted by a ghost warning her of deaths about to come in the city of New Orleans, deaths caused by the same murderer who stole the life of the beautiful ghost haunting her dreams night after night.

At first, Jake is afraid that returning home has simply awakened some of the fear of the past…

But as Ashley's nightmares continue, a body count begins to accrue in the city…

And it's suddenly a race to stop a killer before Hallow's Eve comes to a crashing end, with dozens more lives at stake, not to mention heart, soul, and life for Jake and Ashley themselves.

* * * *

Blood on the Bayou: A Cafferty & Quinn Novella

It's winter and a chill has settled over the area near New Orleans, finding a stream of blood, a tourist follows it to a dead man, face down in the bayou.

The man has been done in by a vicious beating, so violent that his skull has been crushed in.

It's barely a day before a second victim is found... once again so badly thrashed that the water runs red. The city becomes riddled with fear.

An old family friend comes to Danni Cafferty, telling her that he's terrified, he's certain that he's received a message from the Blood Bayou killer--It's your turn to pay, blood on the bayou.

Cafferty and Quinn quickly become involved, and--as they all begin to realize that a gruesome local history is being repeated--they find themselves in a fight to save not just a friend, but, perhaps, their very own lives.

* * * *

All Hallows Eve: A Krewe of Hunters Novella

Salem was a place near and dear to Jenny Duffy and Samuel Hall -- it was where they'd met on a strange and sinister case. They never dreamed that they'd be called back. That history could repeat itself in a most macabre and terrifying fashion. But, then again, it was Salem at Halloween. Seasoned Krewe members, they still find themselves facing the unspeakable horrors in a desperate race to save each other-and perhaps even their very souls.

* * * *

When Irish Eyes Are Haunting: A Krewe of Hunters Novella

Devin Lyle and Craig Rockwell are back, this time to a haunted castle in Ireland where a banshee may have gone wild—or maybe there's a much more rational explanation—one that involves a disgruntled heir, murder and mayhem, all with that sexy light touch Heather Graham has turned into her trademark style.

* * * *

Crimson Twilight: A Krewe of Hunters Novella

It's a happy time for Sloan Trent and Jane Everett. What could be happier than the event of their wedding? Their Krewe friends will all be there and the event will take place in a medieval castle transported brick by brick to the New England coast. Everyone is festive and thrilled... until the priest turns up dead just hours before the nuptials. Jane and Sloan must find the truth behind the man and the murder--the secrets of the living and the dead--before they find themselves bound for eternity--not in wedded bliss but in the darkness of an historical wrong and their own brutal deaths.

About Heather Graham

New York Times and *USA Today* bestselling author, Heather Graham, majored in theater arts at the University of South Florida. After a stint of several years in dinner theater, back-up vocals, and bartending, she stayed home after the birth of her third child and began to write. Her first book was with Dell, and since then, she has written over two hundred novels and novellas including category, suspense, historical romance, vampire fiction, time travel, occult and Christmas family fare.

She is pleased to have been published in approximately twenty-five languages. She has written over 200 novels and has 60 million books in print. She has been honored with awards from booksellers and writers' organizations for excellence in her work, and she is also proud to be a recipient of the Silver Bullet Award from the International Thriller Writers and was also awarded the prestigious Thriller Master in 2016. She is also a recipient of the Lifetime Achievement Award from RWA. Heather has had books selected for the Doubleday Book Club and the Literary Guild, and has been quoted, interviewed, or featured in such publications as The Nation, Redbook, Mystery Book Club, People and USA Today and appeared on many newscasts including Today, Entertainment Tonight and local television.

Heather loves travel and anything that has to do with the water and is a certified scuba diver. She also loves ballroom dancing. Each year she hosts a ball or dinner theater raising money for the Pediatric Aids Society and in 2006 she hosted the first Writers for New Orleans Workshop to benefit the stricken Gulf Region. She is also the founder of "The Slush Pile Players," presenting something that's "almost like entertainment" for various conferences and benefits. Married since high school graduation and the mother of five, her greatest love in life remains her family, but she also believes her career has been an incredible gift, and she is grateful every day to be doing something that she loves so very much for a living.

Discover 1001 Dark Nights

COLLECTION ONE

FOREVER WICKED by Shayla Black ~ CRIMSON TWILIGHT by Heather Graham ~ CAPTURED IN SURRENDER by Liliana Hart ~ SILENT BITE: A SCANGUARDS WEDDING by Tina Folsom ~ DUNGEON GAMES by Lexi Blake ~ AZAGOTH by Larissa Ione ~ NEED YOU NOW by Lisa Renee Jones ~ SHOW ME, BABY by Cherise Sinclair~ ROPED IN by Lorelei James ~ TEMPTED BY MIDNIGHT by Lara Adrian ~ THE FLAME by Christopher Rice ~ CARESS OF DARKNESS by Julie Kenner

COLLECTION TWO

WICKED WOLF by Carrie Ann Ryan ~ WHEN IRISH EYES ARE HAUNTING by Heather Graham ~ EASY WITH YOU by Kristen Proby ~ MASTER OF FREEDOM by Cherise Sinclair ~ CARESS OF PLEASURE by Julie Kenner ~ ADORED by Lexi Blake ~ HADES by Larissa Ione ~ RAVAGED by Elisabeth Naughton ~ DREAM OF YOU by Jennifer L. Armentrout ~ STRIPPED DOWN by Lorelei James ~ RAGE/KILLIAN by Alexandra Ivy/Laura Wright ~ DRAGON KING by Donna Grant ~ PURE WICKED by Shayla Black ~ HARD AS STEEL by Laura Kaye ~ STROKE OF MIDNIGHT by Lara Adrian ~ ALL HALLOWS EVE by Heather Graham ~ KISS THE FLAME by Christopher Rice~ DARING HER LOVE by Melissa Foster ~ TEASED by Rebecca Zanetti ~ THE PROMISE OF SURRENDER by Liliana Hart

COLLECTION THREE

HIDDEN INK by Carrie Ann Ryan ~ BLOOD ON THE BAYOU by Heather Graham ~ SEARCHING FOR MINE by Jennifer Probst ~ DANCE OF DESIRE by Christopher Rice ~ ROUGH RHYTHM by Tessa Bailey ~ DEVOTED by Lexi Blake ~ Z by Larissa Ione ~ FALLING UNDER YOU by Laurelin Paige ~ EASY FOR KEEPS by Kristen Proby ~ UNCHAINED by Elisabeth Naughton ~ HARD TO SERVE by Laura Kaye ~ DRAGON FEVER by Donna Grant ~ KAYDEN/SIMON by Alexandra Ivy/Laura Wright ~ STRUNG UP by Lorelei James ~ MIDNIGHT UNTAMED by Lara Adrian ~ TRICKED by Rebecca Zanetti ~ DIRTY WICKED by Shayla Black ~ THE ONLY ONE by Lauren Blakely ~ SWEET SURRENDER by Liliana Hart

COLLECTION FOUR

ROCK CHICK REAWAKENING by Kristen Ashley ~ ADORING INK by Carrie Ann Ryan ~ SWEET RIVALRY by K. Bromberg ~ SHADE'S LADY by Joanna Wylde ~ RAZR by Larissa Ione ~ ARRANGED by Lexi Blake ~ TANGLED by Rebecca Zanetti ~ HOLD ME by J. Kenner ~ SOMEHOW, SOME WAY by Jennifer Probst ~ TOO CLOSE TO CALL by Tessa Bailey ~ HUNTED by Elisabeth Naughton ~ EYES ON YOU by Laura Kaye ~ BLADE by Alexandra Ivy/Laura Wright ~ DRAGON BURN by Donna Grant ~ TRIPPED OUT by Lorelei James ~ STUD FINDER by Lauren Blakely ~ MIDNIGHT UNLEASHED by Lara Adrian ~ HALLOW BE THE HAUNT by Heather Graham ~ DIRTY FILTHY FIX by Laurelin Paig ~ THE BED MATE by Kendall Ryan ~ NIGHT GAMES by CD Reis ~ NO RESERVATIONS by Kristen Proby ~ DAWN OF SURRENDER by Liliana Hart

COLLECTION FIVE

BLAZE ERUPTING by Rebecca Zanetti ~ ROUGH RIDE by Kristen Ashley ~ HAWKYN by Larissa Ione ~ RIDE DIRTY by Laura Kaye ~ ROME'S CHANCE by Joanna Wylde ~ THE MARRIAGE ARRANGEMENT by Jennifer Probst ~ SURRENDER by Elisabeth Naughton ~ INKED NIGHTS by Carrie Ann Ryan ~ ENVY by Rache Van Dyken ~ PROTECTED by Lexi Blake ~ THE PRINCE by Jennife L. Armentrout ~ PLEASE ME by J. Kenner ~ WOUND TIGHT by Lorelei James ~ STRONG by Kylie Scott ~ DRAGON NIGHT by Donna Grant ~ TEMPTING BROOKE by Kristen Proby ~ HAUNTED BE THE HOLIDAYS by Heather Graham ~ CONTROL by K. Bromberg ~ HUNKY HEARTBREAKER by Kendall Ryan ~ THE DARKEST CAPTIVE by Gena Showalter

COLLECTION SIX

DRAGON CLAIMED by Donna Grant ~ ASHES TO INK by Carrie Ann Ryan ~ ENSNARED by Elisabeth Naughton ~ EVERMORE by Corinne Michaels ~ VENGEANCE by Rebecca Zanetti ~ ELI'S TRIUMPH by Joanna Wylde ~ CIPHER by Larissa Ione ~ RESCUING MACIE by Susan Stoker ~ ENCHANTED by Lexi Blake ~ TAKE TH BRIDE by Carly Phillips ~ INDULGE ME by J. Kenner ~ THE KING by Jennifer L. Armentrout ~ QUIET MAN by Kristen Ashley ~ ABANDON by Rachel Van Dyken ~ THE OPEN DOOR by Laurelin Paige ~ CLOSER by Kylie Scott ~ SOMETHING JUST LIKE THIS b

Jennifer Probst ~ BLOOD NIGHT by Heather Graham ~ TWIST OF FATE by Jill Shalvis ~ MORE THAN PLEASURE YOU by Shayla Black ~ WONDER WITH ME by Kristen Proby ~ THE DARKEST ASSASSIN by Gena Showalter

COLLECTION SEVEN

THE BISHOP by Skye Warren ~ TAKEN WITH YOU by Carrie Ann Ryan ~ DRAGON LOST by Donna Grant ~ SEXY LOVE by Carly Phillips ~ PROVOKE by Rachel Van Dyken ~ RAFE by Sawyer Bennett ~ THE NAUGHTY PRINCESS by Claire Contreras ~ THE GRAVEYARD SHIFT by Darynda Jones ~ CHARMED by Lexi Blake ~ SACRIFICE OF DARKNESS by Alexandra Ivy ~ THE QUEEN by Jen Armentrout ~ BEGIN AGAIN by Jennifer Probst ~ VIXEN by Rebecca Zanetti ~ SLASH by Laurelin Paige ~ THE DEAD HEAT OF SUMMER by Heather Graham ~ WILD FIRE by Kristen Ashley ~ MORE THAN PROTECT YOU by Shayla Black ~ LOVE SONG by Kylie Scott ~ CHERISH ME by J. Kenner ~ SHINE WITH ME by Kristen Proby

COLLECTION EIGHT

DRAGON REVEALED by Donna Grant ~ CAPTURED IN INK by Carrie Ann Ryan ~ SECURING JANE by Susan Stoker ~ WILD WIND by Kristen Ashley ~ DARE TO TEASE by Carly Phillips ~ VAMPIRE by Rebecca Zanetti ~ MAFIA KING by Rachel Van Dyken ~ THE GRAVEDIGGER'S SON by Darynda Jones ~ FINALE by Skye Warren ~ MEMORIES OF YOU by J. Kenner ~ SLAYED BY DARKNESS by Alexandra Ivy ~ TREASURED by Lexi Blake ~ THE DAREDEVIL by Dylan Allen ~ BOND OF DESTINY by Larissa Ione ~ MORE THAN POSSESS YOU by Shayla Black ~ HAUNTED HOUSE by Heather Graham ~ MAN FOR ME by Laurelin Paige ~ THE RHYTHM METHOD by Kylie Scott ~ JONAH BENNETT by Tijan ~ CHANGE WITH ME by Kristen Proby ~ THE DARKEST DESTINY by Gena Showalter

COLLECTION NINE

DRAGON UNBOUND by Donna Grant ~ NOTHING BUT INK by Carrie Ann Ryan ~ THE MASTERMIND by Dylan Allen ~ JUST ONE WISH by Carly Phillips ~ BEHIND CLOSED DOORS by Skye Warren ~ GOSSAMER IN THE DARKNESS by Kristen Ashley ~ THE CLOSE-UP by Kennedy Ryan ~ DELIGHTED by Lexi Blake ~ THE

GRAVESIDE BAR AND GRILL by Darynda Jones ~ THE ANTI-FAN AND THE IDOL by Rachel Van Dyken ~ CHARMED BY YOU by J. Kenner ~ DESCEND TO DARKNESS by Heather Graham~ BOND OF PASSION by Larissa Ione ~ JUST WHAT I NEEDED by Kylie Scott

Discover Blue Box Press

TAME ME by J. Kenner ~ TEMPT ME by J. Kenner ~ DAMIEN by J. Kenner ~ TEASE ME by J. Kenner ~ REAPER by Larissa Ione ~ THE SURRENDER GATE by Christopher Rice ~ SERVICING THE TARGET by Cherise Sinclair ~ THE LAKE OF LEARNING by Steve Berry and M.J. Rose ~ THE MUSEUM OF MYSTERIES by Steve Berry and M.J. Rose ~ TEASE ME by J. Kenner ~ FROM BLOOD AND ASH by Jennifer L. Armentrout ~ QUEEN MOVE by Kennedy Ryan ~ THE HOUSE OF LONG AGO by Steve Berry and M.J. Rose ~ THE BUTTERFLY ROOM by Lucinda Riley ~ A KINGDOM OF FLESH AND FIRE by Jennifer L. Armentrout ~ THE LAST TIARA by M.J. Rose ~ THE CROWN OF GILDED BONES by Jennifer L. Armentrout ~ THE MISSING SISTER by Lucinda Riley ~ THE END OF FOREVER by Steve Berry and M.J. Rose ~ THE STEAL by C. W. Gortner and M.J. Rose ~ CHASING SERENITY by Kristen Ashley ~ A SHADOW IN THE EMBER by Jennifer L. Armentrout ~ THE BAIT by C.W. Gortner and M.J. Rose ~ THE FASHION ORPHANS by Randy Susan Meyers and M.J. Rose ~ TAKING THE LEAP by Kristen Ashley ~ SAPPHIRE SUNSET by Christopher Rice writing C. Travis Rice ~ THE WAR OF TWO QUEENS by Jennifer L. Armentrout ~ THE MURDERS AT FLEAT HOUSE by Lucinda Riley ~ THE HEIST by C.W. Gortner and M.J. Rose ~ SAPPHIRE SPRING by Christopher Rice writing as C. Travis Rice ~ MAKING THE MATCH by Kristen Ashley ~ A LIGHT IN THE FLAME by Jennifer L.

On Behalf of 1001 Dark Nights,

Liz Berry, M.J. Rose, and Jillian Stein would like to thank ~

Steve Berry
Doug Scofield
Benjamin Stein
Kim Guidroz
Chelle Olson
Tanaka Kangara
Asha Hossain
Chris Graham
Jessica Saunders
Stacey Tardif
Dylan Stockton
Kate Boggs
Richard Blake
and Simon Lipskar

Printed in Great Britain
by Amazon

29029720R00071